TRIPPING IN THE VOID

JACKSON COLE, JR.

TO MY MOTHER

PART ONE
A SONG OF SEASONS

He whose face gives no light, shall never become a star.
Eternity is in love with the productions of time.
The busy bee has no time for sorrow.
The hours of folly are measured by the clock;
but of wisdom, no clock can measure.
—William Blake, The Marriage of Heaven and Hell.

CHAPTER 1
PURE AS A BABY

THERE'S something about me people just don't like, because it always gets me into trouble. The teachers either didn't trust, or like me, especially Ms. Chanowiz, my Kindergarten teacher at Saint Catherine's. She had a coffeecake face, a Hitler hairdo, and yelled about everything.

—SIT DOWN, JONATHAN!

—YOU CANNOT PUT GLUE IN HIS HAIR!

—TAKE YOUR FINGERS OUT OF HER NOSE—NOW!

—YOU WILL SIT FACING THE WALL UNTIL YOU LEARN TO KEEP YOUR

HANDS TO YOURSELF!

During recess the boys laughed at me and said I looked like a girl. I had this ridiculous bowl cut and it was long, shaggy and dark red and the ends flipped up like a bird's wing. None of the boys played with me.

During a puppet show, I got a bad belly ache. Sharp, stabbing pains crushed my sides. I never felt pain like this before. It worried me.

Ms. Chanowiz. I have a tummy ache. Can I go to the bathroom?

No, go back to your seat and watch the show like everyone else.

But it hurts and I don't understand—

WHAT DON'T YOU UNDERSTAND?!

My stomach shot up a terrific stream of fruity pebbles and milk all over her green plaid skirt. And that was magic for me.

AAAAAAAAAAHHHHHHHHHHHHHHHHHHHHHH-HHH!

The teacher's aide, Mrs. Newcombe, whisked me away to the bathroom where I finished throwing up. I cried between each wretch. I thought my eyes would pop out of my skull.

I want my Mommy… I can't breathe… My chest hurts…

Mrs. Newcombe rubbed my back until there was nothing left in my stomach. She was such a nice lady. She even waited with me until Pop picked me up at the side entrance.

Okay, honey. I'm gonna go now. You feel better, okay?

Mrs. Newcombe handed me an assignment to take home while I was sick. The assignment was to follow the directions and color the animals based off the color chart. I got the sheet with a Dinosaur. I couldn't read any of it. I needed help.

Just as Pop reached the final step, I spat out the last mouthful of puke, nearly hitting his shoe. I looked up and smiled. I was a pro now.

When I got home I told Ma I almost died from the throw ups. She kissed the top of my head and turned on the TV.

LAND OF THE LOST!

Keep it down Jonathan, she said.

Ma, I have to do homework. Ms. Chanowiz wants me **to** color this but I don't understand what it says.

I handed Ma the paper and she read it over.

Very easy. This is right up your alley Mr. artist. All ya gotta do is color his face and body red and the claws black. That's it.

I looked at the Dinosaurs on Land of the Lost. They weren't red at all. Fuck this.

But they're green! I don't wanta color em red if they're really green, that's stupid.

Jonathan…

She stopped herself and thought about it.

You color that dinosaur whatever color you want.

Ma smiled and handed back the sheet with a box of crayons. I grabbed the green crayon

and colored the dinosaur until the wax shined.

The next week at school…

WHAT IS THIS? OBVIOUSLY, YOU CANNOT FOLLOW DIRECTIONS!

Ms. Chanowiz handed back the sheet.

F

I returned to my desk and put my head down. My face burned with humiliation. I wished I had to puke again, because this time I would've aimed it right at her face.

When I got home, I showed Ma. Sadness hit me so hard I couldn't even cry.

What a bitch! Ma said, and then covered her mouth. You did a great job, honey! You shouldn't have gotten an F. SHIT ON CHANOWIZ!

She grabbed a pen and wrote it out over the Dinosaur's head. I smiled. Ma always had my back when I was a kid. She flipped on the TV.

Ah, look what's on! The Magic Garden!

I ran to the den and hopped on the beanbag. I turned the Dinosaur sheet over and drew the sunflowers I saw on the Magic Garden. They were tall and happy and yellow and they made me smile. I sang along with Carole and Paula:

If you sing for me (la la-la-la-la-la)

I'll sing for you (lu lu-lu-lu-lu-lu)

If you cry for me (ooo hoo-hoo-hoo)

I'll cry for you (boo hoo-hoo-hoo)

If you scream for me (aaaahhhh!)
I'll scream for you (waaaahhhh!)
If you laugh for me (hee hee-hee-hee-hee-hee)
I'll laugh for you (ha ha-ha-ha-ha-ha)
So come on in without a fuss,
'Cause the magical garden is waiting for us...

I never stopped drawing, coloring or painting. I got real good too. I even painted Ma a picture of Jesus for her birthday. I painted a huge sheet of oak tag yellow and left a blank spot at the top. I put a smiley face there.

That's Jesus. He lives in the sun.

Excited about my new masterpiece I ran through the house yelling for Ma.

I checked the kitchen.

And the den.

The living room, and a few closets.

Even under the couch.

I heard voices coming from the hallway. I followed those voices to my parents' bedroom. At first, I didn't understand or recognized the sounds. I got closer to the door. And the voices became more familiar. Sobbing. A muffled, deep sobbing. She shouldn't be crying on her birthday, I thought. Let me surprise her with the painting! It'll make her happy!

So, I kicked opened the door and held it way high in the air like   a   banner.   Ma   screamed, AAAAAAAAAAAAAAAAAAAAAAAAAAAAAAAAAAAAAAAH while wrapped around Dad like an anaconda, squeezing so hard I thought his brains might fall out of his head.

GET OUT GET OUT GET OUT—OH MY GOD!

Ah, for chrissake, muttered Dad.

Back to the old drawing board again, I said without understanding what it really meant. I always seemed to bother them, so I learned how to disappear.

I found the most perfect place for that: the junkyard next to my house. An old place that fixed refrigerators, filled with compressors, evaporators, and small fans. It had a flowery, chemical smell that kind of grew on me after a while. I built my own little community there. Starwars figures, Army soldiers, plastic dinosaurs, marbles and clay. I'd make tiny people out of clay and used marbles for eyes. I sang songs while I worked:

Frère Jacques
Frère Jacques
Dormez-vous?
Dormez-vous?
Sonnez les matines
Sonnez les matines
Ding, ding, dong
Ding, ding, dong

I spent some of my best days there lying on my back, watching the clouds through the trees, or mini-movies on my Fisher Price movie viewer. My favorite: The Lonesome Ghosts with Mickey, Donald and Goofy.

One day I found wild kittens hiding with their mother under a rotted wooden deck attached to the back of the refrigerator junkyard. Sometimes I'd go back there and throw them bits of my leftover lunch. They really seemed to love liverwurst and cheese. One kitten, the blackest one, I named Shadow. It had the prettiest face I'd ever seen. So I thought it would be a girl. She'd watch me make scenes with the figures and paint faces on the clay people. But she never let me get too close. I almost touched the top of her head once... but she ran away.

Must've been around October, right before my fifth birthday, when I noticed Ma wasn't feeling very well for a while. I remember watching her, hunched over the kitchen sink, washing dishes like a madwoman. Sometimes the skin on her hands cracked and swelled from cleaning so much. They'd bleed and I'd help put Band-Aids over the deepest cuts.

Welp, looks like you're gonna have a brother or sister, she said.

She didn't seem very happy or sad, just indifferent. I told her I wanted a brother.

You'll get what comes out!

She dunked a plate in the suds then wiped her forehead.

Back to the old drawing board again, I said to myself and ran next door to the junkyard. I sat between two spinning fans and looked up at the sun. It scintillated through the trees. Soon enough, I fell asleep. When I awoke, Shadow lay sleeping next to me. I reached over and brushed a hand over her tiny back. I thought it was odd she let me pet her for so long. I even kissed the top of her head. One of her eyes sunk deeper into the skull than the other. Kind of looked like a marble. The prettiest, clearest green I ever saw. But, she wasn't sleeping. She wasn't resting. She was dead. It was the first time I cried without being yelled at. The first time I cried without thinking about it first.

I dug a small hole beneath the only tree in the junkyard. I placed her inside with some friends I made for her out of clay so she wouldn't be lonely. I then covered the dirt over her and said goodbye. She was the most wonderful kitten I ever saw.

The following summer, Ma had Maggie and Dad built a garden in the backyard with the plants they'd been growing in the porch all winter. They were big and beautiful with long, thin green leaves. They were even greener than the grass. Dad built a chain link fence around the garden. I thought it must be top secret, because they'd talk real low and whispery when their friends came over to look at the garden. Ma called it the Magic Garden after my second favorite TV show, next to Land of the Lost.

Their friends were always coming and going and Ma'd give them packages from the garden, while Dad was at work painting houses. One of the guys got mad at Ma. He said she weighed it wrong and charged him too much money. He got real loud and scary, but Ma calmed him down and he finally left.

I wore my toy rifle on my shoulder in case one of their friends got loud and scary again. I'd patrol the grounds in my Hot Wheels, riding up and down the long, blacktop driveway.

One day I noticed a man parked across the street in the lot. He never came in. He just sat there, taking pictures. So I posed for him. I got off my Hot Wheels and held my rifle in fighting position. I made a war-face and fired a round into the sky. He got a kick out of it, because I saw him laughing and shaking his head. The next day, I saw him again. He took a few pictures of Ma in the garden. I knew she always wanted to be a model, and loved when people took pictures of her, but something about this guy made me nervous, so I pedaled as fast as I could to the backyard and told her about it. She turned around and peeked down the driveway. She saw nothing.

There's no car, Jonathan. Remember what I said about little boys who lie?

I couldn't remember.

Stick out ya tongue.

I did.

Look at that. Your tongues black! Didn't I tell ya when ya lie your tongue would turn black?

I covered my mouth. I didn't want anyone seeing my black tongue, even though I didn't lie. I just thought it must've stayed black from all the other times I lied.

She told me to get inside and whacked me one on the ass.

The next day, the same thing happened, but he brought a friend. I watched from the porch window. I grabbed my rifle and rushed to the front door. I informed the house about the stranger, but no one listened. So, I decided to take matters into my own hands… again. I stopped him at the edge of the driveway and told him *No strangers allowed!* I pointed my rifle right at his balls.

The taller one had a mustache like my Dad. He laughed and knelt down.

How's your Dad? he asked.

I shrugged. Guess he knew the old man after all.

He's inside watching the Yanks. They're losing and he's really pissed off--

Long legs leapt over my head like a giant frog, I turned upward and watched as he landed, then bolted down the driveway. The camera guy ran around back. I got on my Hot Wheels and   hauled   ass   after   him,   screaming STOPPPPPPPPPPPPPPPPPPPPPPPPPP

Plastic wheels skidding at the end of the driveway, kicking up a dust cloud and through the settling debris the image of Dad, hopping over the fence, and Long Legs right up on his ass chasing after him, and it'd be a long while till I saw old Dad again.

The typical daily routine post Dad:

Ma on the phone, either crying or shouting or both.

Ma on the phone, wrapping the chord around her finger 'til it turned a throbbing plumb color.

Ma ignoring me as I'd be asking her to look at what I drew, or painted for her. Holding it high in her face. The nod, the smile, mouthing the words *looks great* and going right back to the phone.

I painted this wonderful picture with tons of color— yellows, blues, reds, violets They represented how I felt inside, the colors of my soul and she brushed it aside like it was nothing. Like it was some big goddamn joke, so I ripped the painting in half, picked up an action figure off the floor and chucked it in the air.

—The kitchen light exploded. Sparks flew and popped like the 4th of July sky. Sparkling bits of glass covered the table and floor.

—Ma slammed down the phone and those Daddy-long-legs giant stepping two steps for my every five or six.

—Blood red claws swatting… swatting…

—The whooshing wind inches from my neck.

—Two hands bust out the front door, stumbling down the steps, and Nana walking up the steps, carrying heavy trays of lasagna. I hid behind her as the red lobster claws swatted and snapped—

Jesus H. Christ, Trish! He's just a kid!

Get ta your room, Jonathan! I don't wanta see your face!

I squeezed in between legs and ran to my room, kicked the door shut, then banged on the door and yelled and cried and banged until my fists swelled and skin scrapped off the knuckles, imprinting tiny blood droplets in the white paint of the door—

I'M RUNNING AWAY I'M RUNNING AWAY AND NEVER COMING BACK! YA

HEAR ME! I'M RUNNING AWAY AND NEVER EVER COMING BACK!

Kicked and kicked the door, wood splintering and breaking—

WAIT UNTIL YOUR FATHER HEARS ABOUT THIS!

HE'S NEVER COMIN' BACK! HE'S DEAD! HE'S NEVER COMIN BACK NOT

EVER AGAIN NOT EVER!

The wood split. Light spilled in through the crack.

DON'T YOU SAY THAT ABOUT YOUR FATHER! HE'S NOT DEAD! I STILL

TALK TO HIM AND HE'S GONNA HEAR ABOUT THIS!

HE'S DEAD

DEAD

DEAD

Kicking and kicking and kicking the toes swelling and cool wetness filling the sock and pain shooting from the toes up the shins—

I grabbed the Snoopy suitcase and stuffed it with socks and underwear while Ma screamed and cried, Dad's not dead, and I'm an evil, evil little kid.

I squeezed the crystal doorknob and pulled and the light beamed from the dining room windows, eyes down, two hands on the handle, stomping toward the front door—

OH THERE HE GOES, THE EVIL KID, THE BAD, BAD LITTLE BOY, LET'S SEE

HOW FAR YA GET… C'MON… LET'S SEE…

I reached the porch steps, my foot throbbing and pulsing and the toenails stinging and burning from the sweat/blood that filled the sock. My chest heaved and heaved, choking on tears and phlegm, swallowing the phlegm, and then gagging back up thick streams of watery mucus, hanging from lips, splattering globs breaking apart on the cement.

—Ma at the front window, shaking her head, shaking her head, frowning.

—I grabbed the plastic handle, squeezed, and sent Snoopy helicoptering through the air and smashing the front end of a mail-truck just pulling up to our mailbox.

—Muffled screams rattled the glass panes

—Fruit of the Looms and socks rained all over the front lawn.

———

HALLOWEEN!

Ma dressed me as a newsboy from the 20s. Blackened my eyes with mascara. Stuffed an old burlap bag with newspapers, and an oversized turtleneck that fit like a dress. Grandpa plopped a denim cap on my head and smiled his half-smile and held his bad arm close to his ribs.

Maggie was a Flapper from the roaring 20's. Red sparkling dress, white lace tights, tiny shiny black shoes and feathered boa tickling her pug nose and sneezing the runny water out—

ACHU!

Aunt Jan met us in their old neighborhood, in front of their favorite bakery, Ciro's. We filled our bellies with Napoleons and Cannoli's, the sweet cream and chocolate chips washed down with milk then walked from house to house trick or treating before the big contest.

Gram told stories about their town and how it was a witch's

town way back in the olden days. And the villagers hunted them down and burned them alive, and Gram pulled her arms way up high so her claws dangled like weeping willows. I believed every word she said. A cold chill hit my bones.

—Her bright red hair sculpted in a beehive. Stacked so tall I thought her head would touch the moon.

Inside my brain I saw burning, screaming witches, melting alive. Their skin, oozing and bubbling, sliding off their skulls like a hot cheese pizza. Their bony fingers reaching out to touch me—

Ma grabbed my hand

Okay, honey this is the last house and we gotta get ta that contest before it's too late.

Grandpa took my hand and waved her off.

Maggie got restless, so Aunt Jan took her back to the car.

Ma waited on the edge of the lawn.

Me and Grandpa walked up the big wooden porch steps. Each step felt like the biggest step of my life. The house was big and moldy. It had shudders and awnings. The paint was falling off the shingles in thick squares. I stuck my finger under one of the squares and snapped it off. It felt kind of good, to tell you the truth. I could've spent all night snapping off piece of dried paint.

Grandpa pressed the doorbell. It rang like a gong.

—Locks unlocked and latches unlatched.

—The door opened.

An older boy answered. There were two more kids inside, giggling and saying things I didn't understand. They were way older, maybe ten or eleven.

Whatta ya say, kid, the boy asked me.

I answered him inside my head.

He waited…

Welp, if ya don't know the magic saying, then I'll hafta say goodnight—

Grandpa made a funny sound with his mouth. Then wiped the drool with a crumpled piece of toilet paper he kept in his front pocket.

The kids laughed at him.

Okay, you can go now—

Yeah, and take the dribbling retard withya—

I bet he uses that cane ta fuck his old lady cos his dick don't work no more!

AHAHAHAHAHAHAHAHAHAHAHHAHAHAH AHAHAHAHHAHAHAHAHAHHAAHHAHAHA

WHATTA STARIN AT, YA FREAK? GET OFF MY PROPERTY!

OH I KNOW, I KNOW HE WANTS HIS CANDY. HERE YA GO!

Lose pieces of candy pelted us both in the face.

I was afraid to look at him, because he might've been crying.

A large presence moved behind me.

The floorboards shook.

The kids turned into statues.

Gram was bigger, even more Globus as if nobody could ever hurt her. The lines in her face looked as deep as fissures. Her mole glowed under the porch light. She looked indestructible.

TRICK OR TREEEEEEAAAAAAATTTTTT!!!

The kids jumped back.

Is that what you were waiting to hear?!

The boy swung the door closed, but Gram jammed her foot in the door and pushed inside.

WHERE ARE YOUR PARENTS?! YOOH-HOO! ARE THERE ANY PARENTS AROUND HERE? YOOH-HOO!

They're not here—

Yeah, yeah we-we don't have any… any… any…

DON'T HAVE ANY WHAT!

The kids lost their tongues.

DON'T HAVE WHAT?! SPIT IT OUT!

Parents!

Yeah, we're orphans!

Ah-ha! We have something in common, because I too, was an orphan.

Grandma stopped in the middle of the foyer. She rolled her

head around as if something took over her body, then flashed her eyes and said:

Do you know the *true* meaning of Halloween, hmmm?

They shrugged.

Oh, then I'll tell you—

Kids dress-up in scary costumes ta get candy. The end. Now, leave! said the fat one.

Actually, it's a Celtic holiday, my little *brat!* And I am of Celtic origin. Halloween is a day to *honor* the dead, and one must wear these masks to ward off the evil spirits to keep them from possessing LITTLE. BODIES.

Gram poked the tubby kids belly with Grandpa's cane, and continued:

But, you see, I am not wearing a costume… I don't need to… because IIIIIIIIII… ammmmmmm… a WITCH!

The kids roared with laughter.

Okay, great, you're a witch. Now get the fuck outta our house!

Grandma tightened her mouth. Her eyes flashed again. She flung her arms out:

I CHALLENGE ALL THE SPIRITS OF HALLOWEEN NIGHT—

—Lights flickered.

—The bulbs rattled.

I said get the hell outta our house ya crazy old witch!

Yeah, we're callin the cops, ya freak!

clip-clop, clip-clop

clip-clop, clip-clop

clip-clop, clip-clop

—The white door next to the staircase.

—The swinging door that separated the kitchen from the living room.

—A large space between the bottom of the door and the floor.

—A pair of black high-heeled shoes paced there.

clip-clop, clip-clop

Ah, your parents must be home, said Gram.

She inched closer to the door.

Yoo-hoo… she said. Yoo-hoo, helllooooooo?

The shoes stopped.

Grandma swallowed her breath.

Crawling over to the kitchen door was probably the hardest thing the fat kid ever had done in his short life. That was all; that was it. Nothing else to that very day even came close.

He put his face on the floor, and then tilted his head to get a better look.

All the fear of the human mind rests in a door slightly ajar. Especially when there's a pair of unknown Victorian heels on the other side.

Moonlight flooded in the windows and sliced the room, turning it into a dreamy maze.

The fat kid gasped air from his nose—

Th-th-th-that's not… Mommy's… shoes…

A KNOCK cracked through the air

Grandma jumped.

The kids froze, cemented together at the shoulder.

I sunk my face into the turtle neck. The darkness in there was worse than out there, so I peeked back out.

—An old man dressed in black stood in the front door, smiling. His skinny teeth; sharp and frightening.

Hello, Ma'am. Are you interested in buying some LIFE insurance?

The man widened his eyes.

They sparkled just for a moment in the moonlight, red sacks dropped below the lids, as blank as a moon. There was no human thought or feeling to them.

The kids screamed and dissolved into the shadows, much like this crazy fantasy of how I really wanted the story to go. None of it even happened. I got no candy. Gram called us down from the stoop. The kids slammed the door shut. Tears dribbled down Grandpa's face. He wiped them away with the crinkled tissue. Gram hugged him and Ma kissed his head.

We made it to the contest just in time.

They entered me in.

The Scarecrow told me where to stand.

The judges sat at a table, holding pens and writing on paper. It was decorated with bats and pumpkins. Black and orange was everywhere. I saw such wonderful costumes. Plenty of clowns, Disney characters, dead nuns, monsters, vampires, witches, and one girl had the neatest costume I ever saw. A Grandfather Clock. She wore brown tights and brown elf shoes.

I thought she looked wonderful.

Step forward kiddo, said the girl judge with the big, round glasses.

So I did.

Who are you supposeta be? she asked.

Me? I'm a boy.

She laughed, but it was a nice laugh. Her voice was soft and gentle.

I know you're a boy, silly. Tell us about your costume.

I looked at Ma and she made hand signals to pass out the newspapers to each judge.I'm a newsboy, I said. From the olden days.

Then walked up to the table, and handed each judge a newspaper.

What do ya wanta be when ya grow up? the man judge asked.

An artist.

The judges smiled.

What kinda artist? asked the girl judge.

One that makes things, I shrugged. Then looked to Grandpa and said, *Happy* things.

The judges smiled and laughed.

I'm only here for a short time, I told them.

They looked real sad when I said it, too.

But, it's because I have to go to bed soon. So, don't be sad, I'll be back again.

And I bowed.

They clapped and whistled. Ma snapped a picture of me. I still have it.

I never made so many people happy at the same time in all my life. And it was wonderful.

—The judges tallied the votes.

— The clanking chains, howling wolves, and spooky laughs echoed from the speakers.

—Legs and feet pounded the floor to Halloween music, and the laughter, the laughter, the smiles.

—Heads bobbed up from the metal tub of water with apples in mouths.

—Grandpa twirled Gram with his good arm, and spun her round and round.

—Ma placed a blanket on the floor for us. I ate animal crackers while Maggie slept.

Aunt Jan and Mom danced some more and laughed at each other and I laughed with them.

Soon enough, I fell asleep.

Princess Leia woke me up. She smiled, glitter sparkled off her red lips.

Wake up sleepyhead. You won 3rd place!

Ma kissed me over and over.

There ya go, buddyboy! Aunt Jan said. You're a winner!

The Grandfather clock bowed before the judges. She won 1st place. Tweedle Dee and Tweedle Dum got 2nd. The girl judge placed the medal around my head. She knelt down and said congratulations Mr. Artist. You're a winner.

A WINNER

A WINNER

A WINNER

Her lips touched my cheek and I threw my arms around her neck and hugged her like I hugged Mom.

Tweedle Dee and Tweedle Dum grabbed my hand and all us winners marched around the room, showing off our costumes.

Tweedle Dum put me on his shoulders and I raised my arms HIGH

HIGH

HIGH

Their faces whirled together: Grandma, Grandpa, Ma and Aunt Jan.

--The convulsing LAUGHTER,

--the uproarious LAUGHTER shaking my tummy…

and I loved it that way.

I waved and smiled and hung on to Tweedle Dum's shoulders, as he whirled faster and faster. Even the mean guys and witches looked nice and friendly and had warm smiles. The Scarecrow, Tin Man, and Dorothy joined us and whirled together, laughing and cheering, and more laughing. Grandma and Grandpa pointed at me and slapped the side of his leg with his good hand and roared with laughter.

A STAR

A STAR

A STAR I'M A STAR

THE ONLY PRIZE I EVER WON

That was all; that was it. Nothing else after that very day even came close.

———

Grandpa tucked me in that night and thereafter until Dad got home. I was seven years old. Dad had a small apartment built on the side of the house for my grandparents. They only stayed a short time though. I must've been in about 4th grade when they moved out. Grandma said Dad made her feel unwelcome. Besides, her Mom died and left her lots of money. And she saw it all at the bottom of a tea cup.

Look! Look! Look! Come over here, my Patricia.

Ma went over and had a look.

See it? See it?

I think so.

Ma didn't see it.

What do ya see then?

Um, well, that thingy on the side kinda looks like a bull…

Grandma rolled her eyes.

And straight down at the bottom, kinda looks like a— is that an S?

Yes! It's a dollar sign! I'm coming into money soon. I knew it.

Can I look, Grandma?

He has a smart mouth, this one, said Gram. Go ahead and take a peek.

I only see mud.

Ya got mud between your ears, said Gram.

They went right back into a conversation about being rich and what they'd do with all the money, and which family members would get it and which wouldn't.

I sat next to Grandpa at the table and colored in the airplanes he drew. He smiled and gave me the thumbs up. Gram came over, while still talking with Ma—

Look at all these beautiful planes! I love em all!

Gram kissed his head a bunch of times and hugged his face. Grandpa smiled. She never once acted mean to him, not one day before my own eyes.

I thought that was wonderful.

———

I stayed home from school because I had a fever. Grandpa visited and sat on the edge of my bed, smiling his smile. He wore the denim cap from the Halloween contest. He raised his arm and pointed at the airplane pictures I still had hanging on my wall. He gave me the thumbs up with his good hand.

Yoo-hoo! Yoo-hoo! Pattie. C'mon, we hafta go. The kid is sick. Let'm rest, honey.

Grandma smiled and waved at me from the hall. She even

blew me a kiss. I caught it and blew one back. Grandpa pulled the covers up to my chin and mumbled, *Feel better.* I shut my eyes hoping it would help the headache go away, but it didn't. I opened one eye and saw Grandpa standing in the doorway, still smiling that half smile. He held his bad arm with his other hand and vanished into the darkness of the hall.

Later that night, I dreamt of flying my own plane and Grandpa co-piloted next me. Both arms worked. He had on big headphones and gave me the thumbs up as we soared through the clouds, twisting and turning, flying to the sun. I made the plane do whatever I wanted—

NOOOOOOOOOOOOOOOOO! DON'T TELL ME THAT! LIAR LIAR LIAR!

A cold, hard CA-CHING! Over and over the plastic receiver smashed against the phone-box.

NOT MY DADDY! NOT MY FATHER! Ma screamed. Her voice echoed through the wall.

I lay in my bed, warm tears rolling down my cheeks.

The sadness lingered around all year and into the next... The holidays felt empty. Downstairs I heard screaming and Maggie rebelling against something. I couldn't make out what they were saying. I was thankful for that.

C'mon, let's go, bud! shouted Dad from the driveway.

But I didn't want to go anywhere.

Get in the van! I got some place I wanta take ya's!

I huffed and puffed and stomped downstairs, out the door, and over to the van. Gave Maggie a little something—

LEAVE ME!

AND STOP POKIN' YA SISTERS EYE, YA LITTLE SHIT!

But I want to.

SHE'LL GO BLIND!

Dad flung me in the back of the panting van. I landed on some drop cloths. Maggie landed next to me.

After the longest hour drive of my life, we ended up at some stranger's house. It had many acres of property. Furry sheepdog puppies bounced and leapt in the air. Dad told us to pick one out. Deep inside, I always wanted a dog, but never told anyone about it.

—The puppies swarmed around us.

—Biting, licking, jumping on our laps, leaping in the air.

—Rolling on their backs, giving their best performance.

One in particular kept rolling over, begging for a belly rub. Dad rubbed away and must've hit a magic button.

—Streams of piss shot upward, missing his face by inches.

Ah, figures it's a girl, said Dad.

I pointed and laughed— I want *that* one!

His face crinkled, Oh you would!

Over the clunking paint brushes, paint cans, scrapers, and rollers hung on a pegboard, we shouted names into the darkness of the van. The puppy sat on Ma's lap.

SPOTTY!

TARA!

BEAUTY!

FALCOR!

What the hell kinda name is that? asked Dad

Maggie cupped her mouth to amplify: From Never-ending Story!

That's a stupid name, I said.

You're a stupid ass!

Maggie hit my kneecap with a roller.

Ma twisted around and faced us:

HEY! NO TOUCHING EACH OTHER BACK THERE! AND I BETTER NOT HEAR

ANYMORE BAD LANGUAGE COME OUTTA THAT MOUTH, MISSY!

Maggie blew a raspberry off her tongue.

I'M SERIOUS!

Shadow! I blurted out.

Ma and Dad answered: NO!

I hate you both!

Sounds like a goddamn horror movie, for chrissake.

Well I like it!

I pounded my fist against the pegboard with the many tools. A few dropped. One plunked Maggie on the head.

Ow! Asshole!

HEY! IN TWO SECONDS YA BOTH GONNA BE WALKIN HOME! NOW CUT THE SHIT! HER NAME IS GONNA BE ALEXIS. WE'LL CALL HER ALLEY. THAT'S THAT.

Ma had spoken. Dad coughed up a laugh and shook his head.

———

After my fourteenth birthday on a lazy, early Sunday morning…

Start packin' this shit up. We're movin, said Dad.

Why? I like it here!

I don't got time to explain this shit.

Ma stuck her head in:

WE GOTTA BE OUT IN A WEEK. NOW START THROWIN' AWAY ALL THE SHIT

YA DON'T WANT.

FINE! NOW GET OUT!

FINE!

The door slammed.

I chucked my Mazinger robot toy against the door. It broke in many pieces.

YOU BETTER CLEAN THAT UP MISTER! screamed Ma.

I didn't.

I sat in the junkyard one last time, between two spinning fans and looked up at the sun through the wavy boughs. The long rays scintillated through the trees.

I said goodbye to Shadow and left.

————

I started ninth grade at a new Middle School. No one knew me. No one knew me from my old school either and I was fine with that. Large groups of kids scattered about on the front lawn of the school. The wind blew stronger than usual. The buses lined up along the round-about. The diesel smelled familiar. I thought of Shadow.

Two guys stood under the big elephant tree next to the buses. One looked a bit puffy with blonde hair swooped over to one side, and shaved all around into a mushroom. The other guy had the same haircut, but much longer in the front, dyed the darkest black I ever seen. Like feathers of a raven.

They had skateboards under their arms and their clothes were huge, hanging off their bodies. The blonde one lifted his board high in the air then dropped on top of it and landed smoothly.

How'd ya do that? I asked.

I dunno, I just do it. It's called a bomb drop.

How long have ya been doing this?

I dunno, I didn't mark it on my calendar.

He grinned, showing his yellow teeth. It was a dazed sort of grin where he gave the impression he was either high on something or acting too cool to show his honest feelings. Either way, I thought his attitude sucked. I wanted to punch him in the face. But something about him was interesting.

I'm Jonathan, I said.

He flicked his hair off his eyes and said, Chris. That's Jacob.

Jacob was sweating buckets, messing around on his skateboard, pulling off tricks that defied logic. His back foot snapped down on the tail of the board and his front foot slid up and hit the nose lifting all four wheels off the ground. He got pretty high too. I didn't know how he landed without breaking his ass.

What's that one called?

An Ollie, said Jacob. How tall are you?

I dunno, pretty tall I guess.

Jacob, standing on his board, was just about up to my nose.

What grade are you in?

Ninth. Whatta bout you guys?

Both in eighth, answered Chris.

Ya sure ya don't wanta try?

I would like to learn one day.

Chris and Jacob laughed.

You sound like a fregin robot, Chris said.

I'm sorry.

They laughed again.

Whatta ya apologizing for? We're just messin around.

Do some more of those moves, I said.

—Chris snapped the board up and spun it around his arm.

—He caught it on the backside of his hand, grabbed it, and landed on top.

What's up with them 'nut-huggers' man... you some kinda faggat? asked Chris.

Whudya call me?

Chris rolled over and hopped off his board.

I said you some kinda faggat or sumptin?

He stepped closer; his hot breath of sour milk polluting the air between us.

—I shoved him away then threw my arm around his neck, pulling down a headlock.

—Pivoted the hip, shifted weight.

—Chris flew over my hip.

—Both landed on the ground. I squeezed tight, the crook of my arm crushing his windpipe.

Ya give? I said. I ain't lettin go till ya give.

I tightened the headlock and heard a gasp.

Yo, let'm up! C'mon man, he can't breathe, said Jacob.

BREAK IT UP BREAK IT UP LETS GO LETS GO! UP! UP! BOTH OF YOU!

A long, thin teacher with a long thin nose ripped us apart. Dean Franklin. What a pleasure.

Chris dropped like a sack, clutching his throat.

IN THE DEAN'S OFFICE…

Are either of you going to answer me or are you going to sit there staring at your shoes, asked Dean Franklin. I'm going to ask you one more time—

Well, obviously he's an asshole, I finally said. Or I wouldn't've tried to kill'm.

Excuse me. You can't curse here—

Just did.

Chris busted out laughing.

Okay, you're both getting detention. That's it—

AFTER SCHOOL, IN DETENTION…

Chris on one side of a dark class room, me two rows over. In between, a curly haired girl in a white leather fringe jacket and black cowboy boots. I couldn't take my eyes off her. She obsessively doodled on the top of her blue binder.

Hey… hey…

She peeked up.

What's ya name?

She thought about it for a second.

November.

Stop lyin', asshole. That ain't ya name, said Chris.

Mind ya business, dirtbag, she snapped.

Is that your name or not?

Well, it's my favorite song… November Rain.

Her names Cassie and that song sucks… gay-ass glam bullshit music, muttered Chris.

Cassie, unaffected by the insult said, that song speaks to my soul.

That's really beautiful.

Chris covered his mouth and busted out laughing through his hands.

Shaddup dick before I collapse ya neck again, I said.

He clucked his tongue and said, don't cry; dry your eye.

I pictured taking both hands and clapping the sides of his face so hard his brains explode out the top like a thick geyser of meat stew. But his board, the bright partially scraped off, and faded colors on the bottom. The bright neon green wheels, the banged-up trucks, and the clothes; they're baggy and ripped up, but natural. Looked good to me. He's been places and knew things I didn't.

For the remainder of detention I put my head down on the desk. I tried to think of nothing, but Cassie's kicking leg kept appearing in my mind. She'd flex her toes, tightening the calf, the outline of the thighs, curved and full.

Whatta ya a ballerina or sumptin? I asked.

Cassie said nothing. She squinted, trying to make sense of things.

Pointing your toes like that, like a ballerina…

This guy's a freak, giggled Chris.

Mind your business, dipshit.

He laughed again. I focused back on Cassie again.

You have pretty legs.

She finally smiled, but kept her eyes straight ahead. I wondered if her pussy looked like the ones on my Dad's porn videos. If had tiny straight hairs, or long, thick curly hairs like the ones on her head. Could I fit one or two fingers up there? My mouth watered thinking about it; her ankles, calves, sucking, licking, biting around the ankle, up and down the leg. I never did any of this with a girl, yet my mind wouldn't stop thinking—

THINKING

THINKING

THINKING

Dean Franklin dismissed us by 4:30 and I took the late bus home. Chris sat in the back. I decided to sit next to him.

Whatta ya listening ta? I asked him.

He ignored me. I pulled one side of the headphone off his ear. He swatted my hand away.

Gorilla Biscuits.

Lemme listen.

He thought about it, and then lifted one side of the headphones off his ear. I slid next to him and listened.

It's loud, but kinda catchy. I liked it.

Chris kept staring out the window. I knew he hated me, but I didn't want him to.

Hey, can ya teach me how to do tricks on that thing?

He finally removed the headphones and looked at me. A smirk, squinting eyes, a laugh…

Where ya live at? He asked.

Smith Street, down South Ave. You?

Sixth Street. Get off at my stop.

I said okay, and we got off at his stop. I followed him to the two-family house on the corner of Waverly and Sixth. I followed him inside to an empty house. He dropped his board on the hardwood floors and hopped on.

--Snapped the tail down.

--The board flipped twice under his feet.

--Four wheels hit the floor. A dull thud echoed.

Hey, hey, hey… said a pretty lady dressed in hospital scrubs. What the hell ya doin?

Messin around, said Chris.

Well, mess around outside. And who is this?

A sensitive-ass baby, that's who that is, he said with a smirk.

I'm Jonathan.

Nice to meet you, I'm Chris' Mom, Ginny.

Her voice was soft and peaceful.

Are ya a nurse or sumptin? I asked.

Nurse's assistant, said Ginny, glamorous fregin job, lemme tellya.

Chris lead the way back outside. We walked to his garage and it had everything; old skate decks, a dirt-bike, a go-kart with a lawnmower engine, and an overstuffed bunny rabbit named Sam. Sam looked as if he swallowed another bunny. His nose twitched and sniffed my fingers when I touched the cage.

Here, feed 'em alfalfa.

Chris pulled a handful of the stuff out of a plastic bag beneath its cage. He shoved a wad into Sam's face, and then gave the rest to me.

Man, ya ever let that thing out for some exercise?

He'll escape.

You should let'm around the garage at least. That ain't right.

Na, fuck that. He's a hostage.

Chris took off his t-shirt, wiped his pits and flung it in my face.

You stink like a hot bowl of onion soup.

I'm ripe.

Dirty-ass muthafucka. You need a shower.

Chris laughed.

I'm proud of my stink, bitch.

He hopped on the dirt-bike and told me to get on the back. I did. We rode through the dirt trails off his backyard. He pulled a wheelie over a hilly embankment and my stomach dropped through my bowels. But I got to admit, I loved every minute of it.

Hey, how's those nut huggers feel now?! he said, tearing through the woods, coming within inches of hitting the trees.

Halfway up my throat, but I'm just fuckin fine!

Chris gave me one of his old beat-up decks and we slapped an old pair of trucks and wheels on it in his garage. I tried help, but I didn't know what the fuck I was doing, so I just handed him what he asked for and paid extra close attention to everything. And I mean everything. Especially the rumors about Chris. People either hated him, or respected him. He had a big mouth, told people how he felt about him, did drugs, sold drugs, was arrested for drugs, but anytime I'd ask him, he'd always say, they're talkin' shit. Ain't true. The only thing I'd see Chris and Jacob do was smoke a little pot, nothing else.

• • •

Finding new ways to get home faster became an obsession of ours. We'd cut through Harper's Farm, and follow the train tracks south. They'd lead right to our neighborhood. Instead of a half hour, we'd be home in twenty. On one of the hottest fall days I ever seen, Chris and Jacob were way out in front. I lagged behind; just taking in the sun and the hard railroad rocks crunching beneath my feet—

I'LL SPLIT YA SKULL BITCH!

I looked up and Chris was on the ground, some bigger guy pummeling him with punches in the middle of the tracks. Jacob stood off the side, frozen stiff. I ran over. The kid got off him and pushed right through me and kept going. This big Italian kid in a leather coat and cap. The same kind of cap my Grandpa use to wear.

—Chris torn up on the track, twisted, blood oozing from his nose and mouth. My stomach clenched like a fist. I grabbed the biggest, sharpest rock.

HEY WHO'S SKULL YA GONNA SPLIT, faggat!

—The Italian turned around.

—I launched the rock at him. It whizzed right past his face. He threw his hands in the air ready to fight again.

YOU JUST GONNA LAY THERE LIKE THAT? FUCK THIS GUY! I said to Chris.

—The Italian drew closer, hands still up.

—Jacob picked up a rock.

—I picked up two more.

—Chis wiped the blood from his nose and scooped up a handful of rocks.

—The rocks soared through the air.

—One hit on his forehead, splitting the skin wide. He SCREAMED like a bird.

We caught the Italian a few hundred feet down and I jumped on him and he slammed me to the ground in a pile driver. I couldn't breathe. Chris and Jacob pummeled him with punches and dragged him down, throwing more punches and kicks. I kicked him in the head with everything I had. Chris pulled brass knuckles from his pants and cracked the kid's face, bashing up the knuckles of the hands covering the head. Bashing the fingers, the ear, the neck, and spine. Jacob lifted his board and slammed on the elbow of the arms that was waving all around, trying to deflect the punches, the kicks, the heavy wooden deck from breaking his bones, ripping through skin, and cracking on his skull. We kept going till our arms were tired and numb with pins and needles and my foot hurt from kicking (it was like kicking a bag filled with cement)

NO MORE, NO MORE, NO MORE! groaned the Italian, choking on blood and phlegm and tears and Chris gave him another kick and I stopped kicking for a minute and the spit blood-bubbles popped from his lips and I backed up as Chris dangled a loogie from his lips and let it plop on his face, and we left him there, dumped, and headed back home.

FUCK FREDDY… Chris said, wiping his bloodied nose with the sleeve of his hoodie.

He's a faggat. All bent cos I finger fucked his ex-girl.

He looks old as hell, I said.

He's like seventeen. Goes to Bellport, said Jacob.

Next time I see'm I'm gonna cut his fuckin head off with my Army knife.

———

Chris called for me early on a cold, Saturday, November morning. The leaves were golden and yellow and smelled of maple. We skated down the smooth blacktop streets and I had no idea where we were headed. The woods along Creek Hollow Road just kept on going like some strange dream you have no control over; you try with every bit of strength to wake up, but it's no use, because it ends when it's ready to end no matter how hard you try to force out a scream.

We rolled up to this little brick house that popped out of

nowhere. I thought the house looked as if it died long ago. Dried leaves, a broken up porch, and a dirt driveway. I stayed put in the street while Chris went up to the door. He banged several times.

Cassie answered.

Chris waved me over.

I thought about it first. My stomach twisted in spasms and knots. I tried not thinking about it and skated up the walk.

INSIDE…

No pictures. No sense of family or love.

We sat on a mushy, brown leather couch. An ashtray on the lopsided arm, filled with butts, all tipped with lipstick.

I said hi. Cassie said nothing.

Her tits popped out of the sides of her shirt.

Lemme see your cunt, said Chris.

Lemme see your cock, said Cassie.

I turned away, disgusted. I didn't want to see what shriveled mess hung between his pale pudgy legs.

A buckle clanked and unlatched.

The zipper went down.

Mouths popped open. From the corner of my eye I saw Cassie's hand drop a piece of white gum in the ashtray, followed by a slobbering, sucking. My cheeks burned like I had a fever. The dank smell of mold was giving me that queasy, swishing feeling inside my stomach because it mixed with her body odor and some sort of sweet musk. I tried focusing on the records lying on the floor to take my mind off puking. Then her hand slid over my crotch. Chris was cracking up as she shoved her hand down my jeans and squeezed. Took it out and squeezed some more. Rubbed the head, then put her mouth over it and sucked. Her teeth dug into the sides. I almost hit the fucking roof. On instinct, I grabbed her hair and clenched my thighs. Instead of stopping, she went faster, and then choked a little. A deep feeling rushed from my bowels, through my pelvis like a fireball emerging. It kept pulsing and pulsing until I couldn't control it no more. I wanted to laugh and cry at the same time, or jump up and scream. Then it happened. She gagged and her whole body heaved. Cheeks puffed and a line of drool dribbled from her bottom lip. She spat it on the rug and some splashed across an Ozzy Osborn record. It was thick, white liquid. I kept saying to myself, *I hope I don't throw up, please don't let me throw up please don't let me throw up, otherwise this is all she'll remember about me for the rest of her life.*

Welp, that hit the spot, said Chris and laughed his laugh.

My legs twitched from deep inside the muscles. I pulled up my zipper without saying a

word. I felt like a fucking idiot.

Here, said Chris, handing her a tiny baggie filled with white powder.

Thanks.

Cassie opened the bag, dipped a finger in, and then licked it. She smiled.

I couldn't take any more of this crap. The sight of anyone doing drugs made me nauseous. I got up and walked out. My legs shook like marshmallows. I let the broken tin door slam. I got to the edge of the lawn, trying to hold down the puke, swallowing and breathing, swallowing and breathing. Then, they stepped out.

Okay, bye, she said and walked off in the other direction.

My legs would not stop shaking. I was scared they would never stop.

Hey, where she's goin?

Beats the shit outta me, he shrugged.

Doesn't she live there?

No one lives there ya dummy.

Yeah, but there was—

We just go there ta get fucked up and do whatever, he said laughing. I don't know whose house it is… and I don't fuckin' care!

He told me they'd also hang at some place downtown called the Recreation Center, or The Rec. It was an activity center mainly for kids who had no place to go after school. It kept them off the streets, but after a while, the streets became The Rec. They had foosball, ping-pong, video games, a TV room, an aquarium, and a greenhouse with tons of plants. Sounded like a fun place to be.

All of a sudden we almost skated right into something. Chris ollied over it and I just leapt off my board and the board flew down the street and off into the woods. I landed with palms out, scraping the skin off my hands and legs, the pebbles digging and cutting to the kneecap. But Chris' face… his face man… Sitting on my ass, picking the pebbles and debris out of my hands, I refused to follow his gaze. I didn't want to know. At that moment, I didn't want to know anything.

A fuckin baby… just a baby deer, Chris said in the softest voice he ever had since that day.

Look… look at where's he looking you pussy… go see what you guys almost ran over. Just look… stop being a fucking coward. TURN TO YOUR RIGHT. TURN YOUR HEAD TO THE FUCKING RIGHT…

Could've passed for a bag of groceries, maybe a winter coat, or a stuffed animal some spoiled brat tossed out the car in a fit of rage. Could've been any of those, except for the blood, the thick, dark blood gathered in pools. The face was completely broken off; only a bloody pulp with bits of jagged bone and two tiny ears showed.

Shouldn't leave it here… not like this, Chris said.

I agreed.

Every living thing deserves a proper burial, he said.

Chris grabbed two legs and dragged it off the road. The bloody stump scraped over the rocks and twigs and leaves. I followed him into the woods and brushed aside the leaves and then dug out a small space. I rolled the deer in and covered it over with dirt. We turned and walked back to the street. Eyes were so wet I don't know how I didn't smack into a tree.

———

One miserable rainy day I decided to take the bus downtown and check out the Rec. It wasn't bad. Not much doing. A few kids hanging around acting like tough guys, trying not to talk. If you talk too much; you're a faggat. Don't talk at all; you're a weirdo. I'll stick with being a weirdo.

They had this puke green leather couch in the TV room that was held together by duct-tape. A little kid couldn't've been any older than ten watched Star Wars with a few older guys. He kept shooting the screen with a plastic Han Solo laser pistol. Had one of those when I was his age. Felt sort of bad for the kid though. Looked like he's been through some shit. Could've been his dirty face and yellow matted hair. Maybe his ripped clothes and sneakers told me he didn't have a Mom or Dad at home, or maybe they just didn't give a fuck about him. Maybe these guys were all he had.

There was shouting from the arcade room. A couple of guys giving each other a hard time over who's going to play next. My eyes went there and that's when I finally saw her. Cassie. Leaning against the Centipede video game, lips glittering, blood red. Black tights, Keds, and slouch stocks. Acid washed denim jacket all fuckedup with band patches. I watched her ballerina legs, and the way the calves flexed. I wanted to run my hands all over them.

I crept up on her and popped my hip into hers.

Hey.

Cassie smiled.

Maybe she was just real shy. Maybe I looked at her the wrong way, the way guys look at girls when they only want to fuck them. I moved closer and asked her if she wanted to talk, maybe in the plant room. She didn't say anything. Just stared at me. Those eyes. Wide and droopy, sort of half-closed a spider web of blue and yellow; perfect like a diamond.

Ya don't gotta come if ya don't wanta, I said.

She looked at some tubby dude with a rat-tail. I didn't know if that look was to make fun of me or not. He sort of rolled his eyes. I didn't know what to say at all.

She smiled and tapped my hand with her nails, for some reason. I smiled back, and then headed for the plant room. Didn't even bother to see if she was following. Figured if she wasn't I just made a great big fuckin ass out of myself.

When I turned around, there she was. Staring right at me. And of course, I had nothing to say. Not a word.

Where's Chris? she finally said.

Her voice was very smooth and mellow.

Beats the shit outta me. Haven't seen'm all week.

She looked away, and then turned back toward the arcade.

I didn't know if she took a tiny stab at me, I wasn't sure, but the question made me feel about a foot smaller.

I probably should be goin', she said. They're my ride, and I think they're leavin soon.

Hang out with me.

I can't. I'll just see you in school tomorrow. Besides, I live all the way out east and they're my only way back.

How far out east?

Ridge. I moved back with my Dad.

Why?

Cassie gazed through me, her mouth opening and I remember how it felt; soft, wet, and she shook her head, 'no'.

How much doya love Dad?

Pinching an inch with her index and thumb, she said, This much.

How much ya love Mom?

She curled her fingers into an O.

Just hang out with me for a little bit, I said.

Look, I really hafta go, okay? They're waitin' for me. And she left without saying goodbye.

BUT

NEXT WEEK…

THE WEEK AFTER…

THE WEEK AFTER THAT…

I visited The Rec, and told no one. Chris and Jacob spent more time finding skate spots or building ramps or going dirt-bike riding. I had a new obsession: Cassie. She said, yes. No big deal, though. Nothing crazy. Walked through town, ate at the pizzeria, sat on benches, watched people, talked to the homeless. She didn't stand for small talk. Neither did I. Grabbed her hand, played with her fingers, and tickled her palm. She brought a bag of weed. Rolled a joint. Sat besides a lake, and got high. My first time. I hung from the bough of a tree closest to the lake and fell off, got shit-stained with mud.

THE LAUGHING… THE LAUGHING…
THE WORLD SPINNING AND SPINNING…
THE WHEELING SENSATION…

NEXT FRIDAY—

She asked me to walk her a little further than usual. Down by the train station, near Harper's Farm. Just over the hill, you could see Woodland Cemetery. It was peaceful there. Large and hilly with dirt paths and many trees. Pulled out a neat looking little bottle of Evan Williams and went to town on it.

What the hell is that? I asked.

Whiskey, ya dodo.

Cassie drank straight from the bottle, then offered me some. I took a swig. Didn't even think about it. Wouldn't let myself. I just downed a big mouthful and dealt with the burning. It was like someone poured gasoline down my throat. Eyes teared up like crazy. Before I could take another breath, the bottle was under my nose again. A bigger swig this time.

You are the show-offiest muthafucka I ever known, she said. Gimme it back before ya kill yaself.

Cassie drank a good amount of the bottle. She was a professional drinker, I guess. I couldn't get any more down. I got that wheeling sensation again.

I'm so sick of gray, she said looking up. I wanta go ta California… Venice Beach or some shit, away from all this ugliness.

She whirled round and round with the bottle in her hand and laughed. It was the first time I saw her smile. Her face lit up like an arcade, bright and alive.

Looking up at her, half-dizzy, watching all that hair blur together with the headstones, I thought I'd spin right off the earth and up into the sky.

Ya ever tell Chris we hang out?

Nope.

Good. Don't.

She collapsed on top of me and I held on to her; her weight kept me bound to the earth. Nicotine-whiskey hair hit my nose. I never wanted to let go.

We walked through the hilly graveyard, the ass of my jeans held up by her hand. My head on her shoulder, she guided us out and to the train station. It was there, finally feeling less of the spins, less of the pressure in my head and more in control, that I saw her face change again. She wasn't looking at me. I wanted her to look at me, though. Her eyes were off, staring at an invisible something down the tracks.

I grabbed her hand and brought her knuckles to my lips and smelled the nicotine strawberry lotion. Kissed them again. It seemed to make her happy. It must have been nice for her to see me looking at her like that, and know that everyone around saw it too.

Cassie dragged me up the stairs and on to the platform.

The train pulled in and we stood real close to the edge, noses feeling the breeze off the steel. Hands clasped. Her pulse thudded against my wrist.

A conductor's voice came through the speakers and told what train was coming in and where it was heading. I leaned over and licked her mouth. She opened up, and I went in for it, and it was sloppy. I pushed her face harder into mine. Got nothing but teeth. She rubbed soft circles on the sides of my face, and whispered for me to calm down, to really *calm down*. When I did, the kiss got softer, wetter. As she pulled away, spit still attached to the end of our tongues, she licked her lips and backed up. One long legged stride after the other, slow, slow, steady, pointing her toes. I would've fell right on my ass, let me tell you. I got two left feet and not at all graceful. I wanted to be like her, gentle in her grace.

I watched her board the train and immediately run to a window, wave, and wave until I never saw her again. I'd be lying if I said I didn't feel like choking up a few tears, because I did. I would've stayed in that day forever if I could have.

Chris hadn't been at school all week. Our nerves got the best of us, so we skated over after school to see what was up.

Ginny was off. She was *way* off when she answered the door.

Hey guys, Chris ain't feelin too hot. How are you guys holdin up?

We both shrugged, not knowing what she was talking about. First thing came to mind was the flu. I'd be damned if I was going to catch the flu two years in a row. Man, fuck that. Then she analyzed our faces.

You guys… don't know…? she said, a congested sort of sound like something was lodged in her throat.

Neither of us knew what to say or do, so Ginny invited us in and called for Chris. He was lying on the couch, his back facing us.

Tell 'em ta come in, he mumbled.

Jacob led the way into the den. I beat him over to the squeaky recliner and flipped the foot-rest up. Double middle fingers in the air— *fuck you!* Poor old Jacob got the shaft: a rock hard wooden rocking chair. He wanted to beat my ass, I could tell.

Finally, after a minute or two, Chris rolled over and faced us. Red blotches covered his cheeks up to his half-swollen lids.

Cassie fell in front of a train, he said. They think it was on purpose.

Every cell in my body stopped. I went numb.

Jacob did not react at all. His mouth just stayed open. I didn't know how well he knew her, or, before that reaction, if he even knew her at all.

Chris told us a guy named Red at The Rec broke the news to him earlier that week. By the time he told him, she had already been buried. No one at school said a word about it. Not even the teachers. It was as though she never existed.

Small memories came back to me about a girl I only knew for a short while. Tiny pictures of her face. Those spider web eyes. Her hair. Legs. Lips. The redbrick house. What happened there. Her voice. The softness. I would never see or experience any of it again, except in my mind. I knew so very little about her, yet I was going to miss her forever. Even though she was not so nice, I knew somewhere she had a mother who was going to miss her and cry every night.

We never spoke about Cassie again. My heart hurt the most when I sat and thought about how all the fantasies I had of her would never come true.

The three of us walked to the park and watched the sun go down. We didn't say a word for a while. Then Chris got up from the bench and walked to the bay.

I walked up beside him. So did Jacob.

Hey guys, do me a favor, okay?

We both looked at him.

Don't ever leave me… promise?

Ain't a promise anyone could keep. I didn't think that then, but understood it in my heart, so I'm saying it now. I just had no way of saying it then. But I told him I would try not to leave him. Jacob just kept patting him on the back.

THAT SUMMER…

I saw them nearly every day. Chris had a few burnout friends who'd come by and watch us skate whatever parking lot we were at. Sometimes he'd get drunk with them, high, or if he was really in a show-off mood, a little coke. And that's when the fun would happen. We'd watch him tweak out, bouncing all over the place, trying to ollie shopping carts, safety cones, handrails, falling down stairs, laughing that madman laugh. Attempted wall-rides, but scraped his face against the bricks instead of the wheels.

I'd lay off the yayo, said Jacob.

Why? I'm muthafuckin Superman!

No, you're Daffy Duck.

Chris seemed less and less interested in skating. He was *real* good, but his focus wasn't there anymore. The burnouts had his attention. Even Jacob drifted. He linked up with some tall, giraffe looking muthafucka everyone called Monk. Monk was my age and knew nothing. He looked old. Had a mustache by thirteen. Scraggly thin nut hairs covered his face and neck in small patches. He was a hard guy to look at. Oh and he had the most embarrassing laugh, this deep Jolly Green Giant laugh—*Huh-huhhh-huhhh!* Man, he was just awful. As much as I missed hanging with Jacob, I couldn't be there when that muthafucka was around. I didn't want to cause any problems, so I just started doing my own thing. Chris was doing his own thing with these burnout assholes. Jacob was doing his own thing with that mongrel asshole, I figured I'd do my own thing and find myself some new assholes to hang with. And that's exactly what I did. I found Stanley and Walter. No more than a few blocks from my house, skating a launch ramp they made out of some scrap wood from an old treehouse in the woods. They kind of reminded me of Chris and Jacob, but less fucked up. It's funny how you're drawn to the same people over and over again. Stanley was a strange one. He wore this stupid red wool beanie all the time, even in the dead of summer, and always looked constipated. Any type of movement seemed to annoy or exhaust him. Stanley was most content sitting on the curb, rocking the board under his feet, eating a chocolate bar, complaining about everything.

Wintertime: Cold sucks. Fuckin hate the snow. Can't skate.

Springtime: Weather sucks. Always raining. Can't skate.

Summertime: Sun sucks. Too hot. Can't skate.

Fall: Fuck fall. Hurricane season. We get hit with a big one and we'll all be under water.

Can't skate in the water. Fuck fall.

Walter was the workhorse. Never had much to say. Always busy. Never sat still. All that movement and practice made him the best skater around and no one came close but the city kids. He was a life-sized Charlie Brown character. Always in some long striped shirt and the hugest pants ever, so wide I barely saw his feet.

Stanley's mom was a friend to all who entered her house. As Walter put it: she's the Mom of all Moms'. She'd ask everyone to call her, Momma or Big Momma. And it was not because of her size, though she had a few extra pounds, but it was her persona that made her a star among us rats.

Our first conversation and went something like this:

Chickens or Pizza? asked Momma.

Pizza.

Great. You're stayin' for dinner by the way.

She sat on the high curb in front of their house wearing pink fuzzy slippers and a grey moo-moo. Rayanne, a curly haired mouth of braces around my age sat next to her. Momma teased me about Rayanne all the time. Say she was asking for me, that I was a cutie, and all this other bullshit. At first, I never knew how to take her, but me and Ray hooked up a bunch of times and we liked each other pretty much right off the bat, so Momma was serious in a joking sort of way.

It was that FIRST DAY, though… that FIRST SUMMER DAY that really gets me choked up when I think about it. That first summer day we were all together. The laughing, the name calling, the yelling, and bitching. The playing around with Rayanne, the sneaking her off to the bathroom for a feel. She'd show me her tits, her ass (more than a handful of tits and ass for such a skinny girl) touch me over my pants, really teasing the fuck out of me, loving every second of giving me the bluest balls of the year.. The sloppy never-ending kisses. Hearing the horror movies blasting from the den, everyone callings us back out: *Where the fuck are you two?!* The skate video pranks and some kid eating a worm then puking it back up. And Rocky added to the chaos, mule kicking the door closed after he'd come back from taking a leak, and opening the damn the thing when he'd want to, eating slugs and moths and slobbering you with his big Boxer dog slobbering jaws. Too big and muscly to sit on your lap, but he did anyway. And by the time he'd finally get off you, you'd be covered with snot, needle-like dog hairs, and thick mucousy slug droppings, insects, or whatever-the-fuck- else he inhaled from the backyard grass. Man, we had a pissa. I just wish it would've stayed that way because nothing ever came that close, not even to this very day.

———

We skated the handball courts off Waverley Avenue, sometime around Halloween. Chris hung out there with his burnouts, smacking away at the blue rubber ball. He was with a bunch of girls I never seen before. Real fucked up looking, unruly bunch that didn't wash their hair or paint their nails. Me, Stanley and Walter skated on the opposite side of the wall. Chris came over and asked if we had a smoke. He knew we didn't smoke. Fuckin' showoff.

I saw something from the other side of the wall. A cherry red convertible Mustang, one of those 5.0 jobs, creeping up on the grass heading right for the handball court. Just as Chris got to the other side of the courts, the guys in the convertible hopped out. I dropped my board and ran over. What happened next really fucked me up in many ways. As soon as Chris started the volley, Freddy and his boys were all over him. He was on the ground, taking the worst beating I'd ever seen. He covered his head with his hands and disappeared behind a mob of legs, arms, leather jackets, and jeans. It was the last image I remember before getting cracked in the nose. I saw a quick flash of a fist with gold rings then, nothing.

I awoke choking on my own blood and mucus. One of the burnout girls had her hand under my head, hysterical; screaming something about an ambulance and Chris wasn't moving or breathing. The world spun like a merry-go round. The trees, clouds, and people moved backwards with tiny electric dots popping and swirling like I could reach out and grab them. I rolled over and puked.

The EMS workers took Chris away on a stretcher. They had him in some sort of neck brace. He was not moving. The lady EMS worker held an ice bag on my nose. The bleeding stopped, but the pain shot up through my eyes and forehead with sharp, electric zaps. They begged me to go to the ER for X-Rays. I told him I wasn't dizzy anymore. I kept saying *I'm fine*, over and over again. I'd never been to a hospital and planned to keep it that way.

The cops filled out some report. They asked me tons of questions. Whether I knew the guys who beat us down, and I said no. Fear made me say it. I knew if the neighborhood guys found out you were a rat, you'd be nothing but dog piss. Even if you ratted on some faggat thug like Freddy, you'd be a piece of shit, because you just proved you couldn't be trusted. So I kept my mouth shut. I was left with nothing but a potato size nose and swollen eyes. Ma freaked out when she saw me. She said what I expected, *We don't have the money for you to go to the doctors! Is it that bad? It doesn't look that bad, give it a few days and if the swellin' doesn't go down, then we'll take ya. But only if it's absolutely necessary.*

The swelling went down after I popped it back in place. Looked less like a potato and more like a nose, but remained an ugly S-shaped down the bridge. I made sure I iced it up real good to keep it numb. Would have I preferred to see a doctor? Yeah. But it never happened.

I next day I visited Chris in the hospital. Stanley and Walter came, and they wound up befriending him. Not close friends or anything, but I'd hear about their skating stories the days I wasn't around. They all seemed to like each other and I was fine with that.

Chris had a bad concussion and seven stitches in the shape of a lightning bolt on the left side of his face. The skin split right over his cheek bone. Only thing I kept thinking about was that day at the park and what he told us there. His face—

————

After the Freddy incident, we spent less time on the Island and more time in the City. We stuck to this place called the Brooklyn Banks. It had these huge hilly embankments that were smooth and sleek, which made it perfect for skating. The Banks was a gathering ground, a place to get away from a place you hated because you was rejected. Because you was a fuck up, maybe so fucked up nobody gave a rats ass whether you lived or died, but there, you felt less judged and more at home than your own home… if you even had one. And I ain't going to lie; I did more watching than skating. Them city kids were miles ahead in terms of skill and ability, but there was a good amount that stood around like me, asking, wondering, thrilling to the scene, laughing at the normles, bumming smokes, getting high, getting drunk, and doing what they had to do.

Some days we'd take the train, some days Momma would drive us, and we'd take the train back, or Stan's Dad, Pauly would pick us up in his patrol car. Pauly was a homicide detective out of Queens, so Brooklyn wasn't too far away from his job. We rarely saw the guy because he worked such crazy hours, and some days he wouldn't even come home. Oh Mr. Pauly, never serious but always a piece of stone at the same time. Harassing us, busting our balls, horsing around with us. Especially Stanley. He'd throw his ass to the floor and cuff him, pretending he was going down to County for murder or some kind of drug charge.

C'mon, let's go ya little mutterfucker you!

Oh Mr. Pauly, the brown thinning hair slicked back around the ears. The small thin face and dark marbled eyes, that never seemed to blink. He'd squeeze your hand when he shook it and hit a pressure point, dropping you to your knees, then you'd look up, and he'd stare you down, without blinking, still unsure if he was joking or not. He was stronger than us. Seen the dark underbelly of our city. I thought he knew everything. And if it was your first time in his home, he'd show you the photo album of the dead, filled with polaroid's of mutilated bodies, kids our age, purple and blue overdosed faces, some shot-up, heads blown apart looking more like hamburger meat than a real person, and man, death ain't nothing like the movies. More like the dead baby deer, or opossum, or squirrel you'd see torn up on the side of the road. More like that.

I tried to replicate the first summer spent with the new crew, but each following summer was different, yet sort of the same—

More pizza, more Rayanne on the couch, in the bathroom when no one was looking, or knocked-out on the sofa. More touching, grabbing, squeezing, biting, kissing, pulling, her soft belly, the tiny blonde hairs, the warmth of her pussy, the feline odor, the wetness, nervousness, scared, trembling, shaking. Horror movies, more of those, courtesy of Stan, all those fucked up images on the screen just washing over, some blonde demon girl made lipstick disappear into her nipple and Stan's hand tapping the rewind and pause and laughing harder each time he did it. And the food, the food, the food!!!! Fried chicken on Halloween and tons of candy, soda, pork rinds, hotdog barbecues, burgers, extra cheese and pickles, bullseye eggs and Momma and her big, loud circus of energy.

Pizza or chicken?!

Stan would sometimes say, Chinese!

I ain't gettin no goddamn Chinese, Stanley! Momma said.

Wonton soup!

You're not getting any goddamn wonton soup! Pizza or chicken!

Then I'd chime in, Wonton! Wonton! Fuck the pizza or chicken!

And that'd be taking it too far and I'd be biting my tongue—

When Momma shot smoke from her nostrils that meant your ass. That meant you'd better apologize or *else*. Or *else* it could mean no Momma's house for a week. And that meant pure torture because you'd be home miserable thinking about her home and all the fun everyone was having. But that's what happens to guys like me who push things too far, who'd mess with Rocky by flicking his balls. Who'd make bongs out of the leftover plastic soda bottles and stink up the house with pot smoke. Who'd get caught feeling up Rayanne on the couch, her legs spread to the world. Who took on Walter and Stanley in a wrestling match upstairs in Stan's room and wound up pummeling them through the floor. The only thing that saved Walt from plummeting to a broken back was a thick electrical cable that acted as a stirrup; his ass sitting upon it like a swing. The wood bits and insulation in Momma's deep fryer, afloat. Her looking up at this, cigarette between the teeth, spatula in the hand—

WHAT THE HELL IS THIS?! DIDN'T I TELL YOU JERKS THERE'S A SOFT SPOT IN THE FLOOR UP THERE!

Sorry!

SORRY?! WELL SORRY'S NOT GONNA FIX THAT HOLE BUCKO!

This was *her* home and that meant—

TEMPORARY BANISHMENT!

Then you'd learn. I had to learn my boundaries with her. And after the banishment, I'd come back over when the guys weren't there so I'd feel less like an ass, and it'd go something like this:

Hi Momma… I'm sorry. Can I come back?

Hey guy. Of course ya can. Come inside.

Then you'd have 'the talk', and it'd go something like this:

I love ya's ta death, but ya's gotta be respectful, okay? It's not just you, so don't take this personal. It's Chris, Jacob, and even Walt can be a little pest. Ya's can't break the place up. I only got one house.

Okay, I'm sorry. Won't happen again; promise.

And that was that.

———

Chris' Mom fell in love with the Post Master. A hefty German named Marv.

He had shotguns, bee-bee guns and a shit-ton of knives. He a was big fun guy. Real swell. He taught Chris how to hunt and he got his practice in by picking squirrels off the trees in the back-yard. No shit. I popped over one time around early April and found Big Marv and Chris skinning the squirrels at the picnic table. Marv held up a dead one and showed me how it was done. Went something like this:

Okay, now watch me. A single cut opens the gut, and see all this here? Those are the entrails. Ya remove 'em like this.

He pulled them out with his bare hand.

Then, cut the head and feet off, like so. Then pull the hind legs out under the skin through the gut cut, like this... once the hind legs are out, rip the hide off.

I watched the entrails slide into the bucket. The blood was dark and slimy and the intestines were like knotted rope. I was curious about how it tasted, so I ate over that night. Tasted like pork but smelled like rotted plants. I couldn't get through it. I bit down into something hard and indestructible. Probed the inside of my mouth with a finger and pulled out a bee-bee. Afterwards, my back tooth felt loose.

BUT BOY, THAT CHEVY TRUCK HE HAD WAS A FUCKIN MONSTER

He only used it for upstate hunting trips and when he'd be working, Chris would take the keys and go joyriding, bringing whoever happened to be around with him. He'd take that grey

Chevy machine to a place called 7 Sisters, a few blocks away and the Sister had big-ass rollercoaster roads that had at least a three hundred foot drop from the highest hill. But anyway, he took us out in that thing I kept my eyes closed and thought my bowels would rip right through my body, flipped off my ass, yelling and screaming and when I finally opened my eyes, and saw all that road flying at us like we were going to flip upside down, I heard Jacob repeating, *Oh shit, oh fuck, oh shit, oh fuck,* then pissed himself through his pants and Stanley yelled *Geroooonimooooo* and Walter showed no reaction until we hit maximum speed down the three hundred footer, and, the most gut curdling whistle-scream-thing I ever heard in my entire life came out of his throat. And he held that scream until the truck stopped. When we did, he turned to Chris and said in his nice-guy voice: Let me out please so I can vomit. He didn't. Instead he sat on the curb and pulled his shirt off, drenched with sweat, trembling like a Chihuahua. Man, it was a pisser… wish you could've seen it.

WEEKS LATER…

I'm sitting in my room, doing nothing, probably counting the little squares on the ceiling, when Ma bulldozed in and handed me the phone without saying a word.

I put the phone to my ear and heard a heavy breathing man on the other side.

Chris had an accident with my truck, said Marv. He's in a coma. Don't know when or if he's gonna pull through—

He began sobbing and moaning.

Fucking Chris. I was sick of it. Sick of Chris and all his fucking drama. All his crazy tough guy bullshit. One minute he's getting his brains beat in, comes out of it with nothing more than a scar, and now the fuckhead smashes the truck up and he ain't going to make it, or maybe will make it or wind up being a vegetable, shitting his pants like a baby. The roulette wheel stopped. Said, not this time. Fuck him. Burn in hell. I don't even care. That's what I was saying to myself. All of that. And the fuck if I knew what Marv was rambling on about over the phone, I think I just hung up.

Ma wormed her way into my room. I saw her from the corner of my eye. She whispered something about something and said sorry and she was on Dad's phone with Ginny talking about it and Ginny's hysterical, blah, blah, blah… Then she was saying something drugs… drugs…. *Did you know he did drugs? Do you do drugs? Tell me, I'm your Mother and I need to know!* I just told her to get the fuck out and leave me alone.

GET OUT!

And Stanley called me, and all he wanted to know was whether I wanted to hitch a ride with him to see Chris at the hospital and I just…. I didn't want another hospital visit with Chris. I didn't want to hear his name and hospital in the same sentence ever again and I couldn't control myself and I just said a bunch of shit I didn't mean to say, it just flew out of my mouth and it was ugly… Whatever happens to him, happens. Whether he lives or dies, I said I didn't care. And that was really all it took. Stan hung up and…

I couldn't pull myself off my bed.

I couldn't talk about it.

To anyone.

I took both of my fists and screwed them into my temples until I had double vision. I dug my nails into the sides of my face and scratched until the skin shaved off under my nailsssssss!!!!!!

That summer was the slowest summer I ever remembered. The humidity was killer. Hung out with Alley in the back porch, just staring at the yard, watching the birds. Watching Maggie skip rope with her new purple sparkling jump rope. Nothing else doing. A can of Skoal left out on the wicker table. Examined it for a bit. Went inside. Checked the cupboards for snacks. Empty. Came back outside. Opened up the Skoal, inhaled. Cherry tobacco. Seen Dad sucking on this stuff a bunch of times, spitting out the juices in a plastic cup. Something to do. I scooped some out and stuck it on the inside of my lip. The cherry flavor puckered the mouth and I dribbled a little off my tongue, watched it sway and break apart, and then swallowed. Felt like a burning ash hit the back of my throat and I puked in the bushes and some bits splashed up on the side of the house. Looked like coffee grinds. I grabbed the garden hose and cleaned the puke off the shingles. The spraying water hypnotized me and so did the mini rainbow coming off the mist. I saw Cassie walk through the mist and wipe the water off her face, her hair, eyes spattered with mascara and she took my hand, lead me into the hospital room where Chris was lying on the bed, facing the wall, and everyone's around him glaring, especially Marv, saying with his eyes, *should've been you* and Ginny saying with her eyes, *Your whole family's no good and you're just like them, anyway.* And Jacob and Walter saying with their eyes, *We're better off without ya and no one ever liked ya* and Stan and Momma hate me so much they couldn't even talk—

Then Cassie takes me out of that place and we're down at the beach, hugging, and it felt good, like nothing mattered. Nothing. None of this. Just me and her and knowing I could go back to Stanley's or Chris' whenever I wanted and hang out and be chill and things would be like the olden days. Why can't I have that back again? *Big whiney fucking baby. Grow up,* I told myself and I even say it now.

Alley kept yelping from the back porch. I dropped the garden hose. The rainbow vanished and so did Cassie. So I checked on Alley and she was, squealing, nipping at her ass, and dragging it on the floor. The fur was bitten away and the skin, red and swollen, yellow liquid dribbling from the cracks. She lunged at me and growled when I got too close. I yelled for Mom.

You see, some summers we couldn't get her groomed because of the money. Ma would clean her as much as she could, and even shaved her down, but the flies still got at her. They laid eggs in and around there and maggots grew into thick, fat, sacks. They got deep in her flesh and caused an infection. The thick, yellow liquid oozed and dripped and it smelled like rotted meat. The flies buzzed. The buzzing rang in my ears like a terrible headache.

We brought her down to the Animal Hospital but had to borrow money from Aunt Lydia because they were having problems with the bills and mortgage and anyway, they gave Alley shots of antibiotics and the vet cleaned out the wounds, by draining the infection, then sewing the skin back up.

Ma bleached the entire back porch and Dad helped. They wore Dad's painting masks because of the fumes. Alley slept in my room for the rest of the week.

The morning before the first day of my senior year, I decided to take a walk by Chris'. I stood out there for a while, remembering. Then Marv flung the front door open and flung his big arms in the air, like goddamn Leatherface. He told me to come inside, all warm and fuzzy and friendly. Stunned by this because it didn't match what I saw in my head. I shrugged. He walked me in. I felt like I was floated there on a cloud in the sky.

The hospital bed propped up in the middle of the living room. He faced the TV unaware of my entrance. I heard the toilet flush. Ginny came out and smiled. I smiled back and floated over to Chris and tapped him on the arm. He took a big suck through a straw and put down a Ronald MacDonald glass. Some mysterious frothy liquid bubbled in there, then he finally looked up.

Heyyy… there he is! said Chris, laughing.

Something wasn't right. His eyes were distant and droopy.

I missed ya. Take a seat. Whatchu been up to?

Marv pulled over a rocking chair for me. I just rested my knee on it.

Not much, I said.

Ya see this? Ya this one? he said, laughing and pointing at the TV.

Happy Days on the screen. The Fonzie walked into a Halloween party dressed in his typical Fonzie outfit except for a thin black mask that covered his eyes. When everyone recognized him, he was blown away.

Like we didn't know it was him, said Chris, giggling.

He went back to drinking his frothy shake. Pill bottles everywhere next to this bed. I couldn't stop staring at them. I wondered if he had to take those pills for the rest of his life. Then, Ginny came over and hugged me.

I'm so happy you came by, she said. That beautiful smile radiated.

Chris kept cracking up at Happy Days, even the parts that weren't funny. So, I finally sat down on the rocking chair, popped out the footrest, and laughed at the unfunny parts with him. I listened to Marv say once Chris can walk again, he's taking him upstate hunting. Then, a small piece of Chris came back.

Nah, he said in his usual voice, and laughed.

Ginny asked me to stay for breakfast. She made pancakes and sausage. I could never say no to that.

As Chris turned over to hand Ginny the empty Ronald glass, I saw the left side of his face. Largely pink mottled with brown and white patches of see-through skin. His left eye sagged into the old lightning bolt scar. He caught me staring and smiled and dropped a fist on the side of my thigh, hitting the perfect spot for a Charlie horse. He always knew where to hit me.

I was too embarrassed to look anyone in the eye because of what I said to Stanley. I knew it got back to him, with his big ass mouth, but no one said anything to my face. None of the guys ever tried calling or coming by, so things just kept feeling worse. If anyone should've been really pissed off it should've been Chris and his Mom, but they weren't. I think Stanley said a bunch of bullshit after we got off the phone and everyone just took his word for it— no matter how much he probably exaggerated—and believed him like a bunch of mindless fucking idiots. I mean I would've apologized to them too for saying fuckedup things about Chris, but no one gave me a chance.

SENIOR YEAR—

First day I saw Jacob. I said, whassup, and he walked passed me. I saw him later that day at his locker and started talking to him like nothing happened. He nodded and smiled in his nice guy way then walked off without saying anything.

Spent lunch in the library. Reading books I hated because there was nothing else around. Read some book Franny and Zooey but I didn't know any kids like the ones in the story, although I fantasized about being rich and having friends like that, because they sounded smart and sophisticated, but I didn't understand them—

EVERY DAY THE SAME

EACH CLASS NO DIFFERENT THAN THE NEXT

Enrolled in drivers-ed, passed, took my road test, passed after 2 tries.

For my 17th birthday, Nana and Pop surprised me with a rusted, metallic blue 1989 Cavalier. It was a used car. Had many dents in the body and missing hubcaps, but it was all mine. I was thankful for that.

———

DECEMBER—

Ma at the kitchen table, staring into a cup of tea. I thought maybe Grandma came by and gave her a bum reading or something. But now, thinking back on it, I wish that were true. Words don't hit so hard as does *the* happening. As does *the* result. As does *the* physical act of doing it. And we did it. We had to. No choice. Evicted by NEW YEARS. The Sheriff came. Didn't even have time to pack everything. Same as before. Left mostly toys I hadn't seen since childhood. The junkyard toy soldiers. Left them. There. It hurt my heart like Cassie's train did.

Grandma helped a lot. She actually found us a place to rent in Seaville. It's a nice town. Real clean and pretty. A small town in the middle of some not-so-nice towns.

Dad knew this guy Louie who owned a small moving company. Apparently Louie owed Dad money for a painting his kids rooms last year, so he compensated by moving all our big pieces for free. And we had a lot of big pieces: armoires, couches, recliners, TV's, TV stands, beds, and one long, long, very old antique dining room table. All mahogany according to Mom, and weighed a couple of tons. Been in her family for three generations going back to Ireland. The legs had feet with large claws. A very dramatic piece, it was.

So, I followed the paint van. Dad rode with his worker Timmy. Ma rode with Gram. Maggie was with me, and she did not say a single word the whole way there. And I was fine with that. Wasn't very far from our old place, maybe five miles or so.

We pulled up to another new house. Two stories high. Another rickety old looking house with banged-up white shingles and black shudders. Small front yard and a two-step cement porch, with an iron hand railing that seemed oddly out of place. Inside was like the outside—old. Dusty hardwood floors, the many stairs leading up to the new bedrooms. The many stairs leading down to a moldy basement. There was a screened-in porch. They somehow found another house with a back porch. Alley ran around, sniffing the air and the floor and the bathrooms— one half bathroom downstairs, and one full bathroom upstairs.

Timmy hurt himself moving my bed up those stairs. He banged his elbow turning the corner in the hall—

It's my painting elbow! he said, eyes tearing up.

I didn't see Timmy for the rest of the day. Dad said nothing about it. He just seemed more annoyed, ordering everyone around and where to put things.

It's gonna take months ta go through all these boxes of knick-knacks! Ma said, blowing smoke out her nose.

Hadn't seen her smoke since I was a kid, and even then she didn't smoke much. And there was the pack of smokes on the dining room table. I swiped one. Found a quiet spot in the new back porch and lit it up.

My mouth tingled and a calm warm feeling filled my body in the dusty light.

The fluttering in my belly, the fumbling fingers, the froth on my tongue, the water in my eye, the bulge in my pants, the itch in my soles, the whoosh of my wind, the pain in my breath, the cold in my lips, the fog in my brain, a loop of my conscience, the replay of events, the tic of my jaw, the crack in my neck, all come swooping forward on the exhale.

———

I began a new school after the New Year. I had the choice to finish at my old school, but I felt nothing for it. I met with a guidance counselor my first day. A drunk lunatic of a man with white hair like a fluffy cloud. He had a hard red face and sharp nose that always seemed leaky. He would scratch and pick away at that thing. Looked just like a carrot.

Anyway, he showed me around campus and introduced me to this real pretty girl, who he said was "garrulous" and sweet.

Her name was Shannon O'Connor.

She was clean and alert, and when she talked she sounded like a teacher. I really liked that about her. Sort of intellectual sounding. Had one of those little turned up noses all covered with freckles. That really drove me nuts for some reason. I thought she looked more like a Catholic school girl. Knee highs and penny loafers. Plaid skirt and a white button down. Some kind of sweatery thing with buttons that hung off the shoulder, and this brown leather bag, probably filled with mysterious shit women are always carrying around with them. Funny thing, she didn't wear any makeup. Don't think she needed it anyway. She had the prettiest, straightest teeth. Made me afraid to smile, with my fucked up mouth. What a dirtbag I was compared to this beautiful creature. Unruly muthafucka. But, I was… fine with that.

We compared schedules and found out we didn't have one single class together. She faked being upset about it. I didn't care. McCray vanished somewhere in the hall. Didn't even say goodbye or nothing. Just sort of vanished.

I kind of felt bad about myself when I looked around. I didn't look like these kids. They wore expensive clothes and had nice haircuts and white smiles. They kind of looked like they'd be future politicians or something like that. Shannon asked me to walk her to class. She seemed to know everybody, introducing me to this one and that one, but none of them said hi or anything. I was used to that.

This one girl, Tracy, with ridiculous blonde puffy hair, kept on talking crazy like a tornado. I was going to be late to class. So, I just shot my voice right over hers—

Hey, meet me in the student parking lot after school, okay?

Shannon smiled and squeezed my arm but didn't say whether she'd be there or not.

Anyway, class was class. I picked up where I left off at Buffalo. I only had four classes to get through, and if I maintained a C average, I graduate. I felt good about that. The only problem was, everyone seemed to be giving me the stank-eye. I made pretend not to notice, and told myself I was being a hypersensitive little pussy, but my stomach told me otherwise.

I didn't want to be there. It was a small slice of torture.

So Shannon wound up meeting me in the student parking lot.

She asked me if I wanted to go somewhere with her. I was like, sure.

So I followed her fancy Volvo to the other side of town, to some tiny beach/park thing. There was a small strip of beach you could spit across, and the ring of brown bay and skyline held a thin slice of light blue the townies called 'Fire Island'.

It was windy and cold and kind of grey. I pulled up next to her in the parking lot. She hopped in my car and told me to turn up the heat. That's like something Ma would do, telling me to turn up the heat. She was either too cold or too hot and was always fussing with the thermostat. The lady was never comfortable a day in her life.

Anyway, Shannon rambled on about how this beach was her favorite place, etc., and how during the winter everyone got together and had bonfire parties there, etc., and her lips, pink, wet, a tongue licked the upper, teeth bit down the lower, and I wanted to suck, kiss, bite, take the bottom lip into my mouth, taste — just a little—of her salvia, so I did. Got close enough for a taste. She opened her mouth and I held my lips on them and grabbed her hip, squeezed, a moan, a soft one, though. Kept my hand there and squeezed harder, she bit down and the blood dripped onto my tongue and I sucked hers—

Then, all of a sudden, she pulled away and said she had to go.

I asked her at least ten times where but she kept repeating the same thing.

When someone's lying and I know they're lying, it makes me feel sort of sorry for them because I see how embarrassed they are knowing they told a lie, and their face gets redder, and they look everywhere else except your eyes.

Anyway, she gave me the best kiss I ever had.

That was all; that was it. Nothing else to that very day even came close.

Bye-bye pretty girl.

The next day, or maybe two days after, I'm not really sure, but, I was standing outside the cafeteria, by myself, eating a cookie and drinking a bottle of soda, when this hairy asshole of a guy came lumbering over. He looked old, but he wasn't. He was shorter than me, but powerfully built. He wore a V-neck sweater and chinos, like something I'd find in my Grandfather's closet.

He didn't get too close, a few other guys hovered around him.

You hang out with her, you talk to her, you even *look* at her again and I'll *fuckin* kill you!

His voice silenced the entire area. Shannon just 'appeared' behind him like some fucking specter, and gently snaked her arm around the chest, trying to pull him away. I looked right into her eyes while I said—

Then fucking kill me, and shrugged.

But I said it loud enough without shouting it.

If he would've taken one step closer I would've bashed my soda bottle over his goddamn head, and wouldn't't've felt the least bit bad about it.

Then McCray staggered over and tried to calm me down, but I walked away. I wasn't about to take advice from that drunk old fool who's head looked like a nimbus cloud.

For the rest of the week, I ignored the stank-eyes, and the fact some random asshole jock slammed me into a locker. I guess it made him feel good.

I really started missing the old crew. I even mailed Chris a birthday card and included a letter apologizing for not coming by as much. He never wrote back, though.

So I felt real bored and lonely one day and decided to drive to Stanley's, but I parked a few houses up. Across the street was the same old broken down car at Bob's brick house. The car must've been from the 20's or something. It had those big spoked wheels and headlights that looked like bulging cartoon eyes. I remembered standing there with Stanley and Walter a few years ago.

I hate that car; it's ugly, said Stanley.

Whuddaya gonna do about it? I asked.

Stanley shrugged, Throw a rock at it.

And he did. The rock dinged off the rusted bumper, hit the car next to it, and set off the alarm. Ah, those stupid random memories that come soaring at you like bird shit on a windshield.

I walked up to Stanley's and stopped at the front door. The big door slightly ajar. I pressed my face against the screen and gave it a tap. Didn't look like anyone was home.

Come in! yelled Momma.

I wanted to run, to run and get the fuck out of there and drive off before she saw me. But her shadow materialized before me in a ring of smoke. I walked in and there she stood in the middle of the den, cigarette hanging from her mouth. My feet wouldn't move. I felt like a fucking idiot.

Hey, guy… howya been? she said, in a slow, dry voice. Her face still soft and warm.

I'm okay, I said.

She told me to sit down with her at the dining room table.

She pulled up an ashtray.

Without even thinking about it, I took out a smoke of my own and lit it up. It's become such an easy habit, like biting my nails.

She frowned.

Not very becoming of you, said Momma.

I know, I said.

I couldn't look at her. I wouldn't talk for a while. The cigarette ash got real long before finally flicking it in the ashtray like an adult.

Do you hate me? I asked.

Noooooo… she whined. But sometimes I hate ya face when ya pissin my dog off! she said, laughing.

But, I don't hate'cha.

Do the rest'a the guys?

Well, they're not *thrilled* withya— that's fa sure.

I went to ask another questions, when—

ROCKY! Get your butt down here! Ya gotta visitor!

The door from upstairs opened and slammed shut. Then four paws tramping from above, then rolling down the stairs and into the den. He froze the minute he saw me at the table. His ears pointed upward.

I said hello and called him over.

Rocky was reluctant, but came over.

I put out my hand. He sniffed it then licked my palm. It tickled.

I miss you, I said and looked right at Momma. She smiled, blowing smoke out of her nose. I could never do that. Every time I'd try, the smoke would burn my nasal passages and my eyes would tear up something awful.

I miss ya too, guy… *sometimes.*

Rocky started popping his jaws and leaping in the air at something I couldn't see.

Get it! Get it, Rock! said Momma in her little kid voice.

Rocky popped his mouth again and caught a flying something.

What the hell was it? I asked.

A moth; he hates them things.

Little bits of moth powder fell on his nose. He lapped it away, then sank down at Momma's feet and blew air out his nose the same time Momma blew smoke out of hers. Maybe spiritually aligned? I heard my Gram say that once and I didn't know what it meant up until that moment.

Just then, Rayanne whirled through the front door like a hurricane, kissed Momma and plopped down in the chair next to me.

How was school today? asked Momma.

It was good, but I hate *everybody* there.

Momma laughed her laugh.

How's your new school, Jonathan? asked Rayanne.

I shrugged.

Fine, but I hate everybody there.

She laughed, then turned to Momma and told her some crazy story about this Jeanette person I never heard of. I couldn't believe it, though. She really didn't seem that pissed at me at all.

I asked the whereabouts of Stanley and the guys and Momma said probably skating the steps at the Bay Mist Ferry's.

So I decided to take a trip down there. The lot was empty. I kind of felt that way too.

———

I would see this guy Ernie who lived across the street every so often. He was a junior, sported a blonde Kennedy cut, and was all neat and clean looking like the typical Seavillian's. He would never listen to a band like Mercyful Fate. He was more of a Billy

Joel sort of guy. I'd see him around school too, and he'd nod his head or give me a salute.

He was alone most of the time, but every so often, I'd see him with this tall, lanky guy who looked like he hated the world. He had this scabby red face, and was always picking at it, ripping off the scabs and flicking them away.

Anyway, one night I saw Ernie sneaking a smoke on the side of his house and thought I'd finally break the ice. So I walked across the street and called him over.

We stood there, freezing our asses off, but even through the chattering teeth, we ignored the cold and just kept on talking, mainly about girls and stuff like that. He told me about this Marylou person he fucks on the down-low. She goes to some private school, Saint something-or-another, and she lets him do whatever he wants to her; cum on her face, her tits, her ass. *Anywhere*. She'll do *anything*. Said there's a treehouse in her back-yard and you could see right into her bedroom from there. Told me to come down one day and watch him get up in her guts from the treehouse. I told him I'd have to think about it.

After that night, he'd stop over and have a smoke with me. I'd crack a window, sit on my desk, and Ernie would flop on the bed.

Sometimes we had things to talk about, other times we didn't, and just enjoyed a smoke. The newest story was Marylou made him watch her piss on her bedroom floor. Right there. She just pulled her draws down, squatted, and pissed. Said it really turned him on. I thought he had more problems than I did.

Anyway, somewhere around mid-March, I was sitting on my desk, taking a break from homework. Not really thinking, just sitting there, hypnotize by an invisible mark on the wall. Then Ernie busted in and flopped on the bed like a fish.

Gotta smoke, man?

Here ya go.

I handed him a smoke. He told me some kid Rugo was having a few people over and he was just up the road from us. I wasn't expecting the invite, so I told him, no. I didn't even have to think about it.

Oh, c'mon! said Ernie. Whatta ya a bear in hibernating?!

I like it this way. It's peaceful.

You're hiding, he said. I know it, you're hiding.

Hiding? I ain't hiding from shit.

I hadn't told him or anyone else about the cafeteria incident. But I'm sure he found out. Seaville's a tiny, tic-turd of a school. Word must've gotten around about the new kid hanging with this slick-dick of a jocks girlfriend, even though I had no fucking idea she had a boyfriend.

Glen Davis, said Ernie, as if he could read my mind. Heard all about it, and he ain't gonna be there.

He looks like a hairy nutsack, I said.

Rugo don't hang out with *those* guys.

I gave him a look.

Ernie got all hyperactive about it, fumbling over his words and animating like a cartoon.

Ya gotta give people a chance, man. Whatta ya gonna do? Hide up here till June? For what? For what?

I had to think about this for a moment.

I just don't fit in with these fuckheads, I finally said.

Listen ta me…

Ernie cupped his hands and spoke through them like a megaphone. They. Don't. Care. Now, c'mon, let's go.

Ernie got up and walked to the door. He waited there. I stayed sitting on my desk, finishing my smoke.

He flicked his head and motioned toward the hallway.

C'mon, he said again.

His eyes told me he really wanted me to come, but my stomach told me it was a bad idea. As much as liked being alone, I felt the need to finally break-out. I had the urge. The urge to prove to myself I was being too paranoid and hypersensitive about things. The urge to maybe make a few friends like the old crew and make more memories… Maybe there was another Momma, or Stan, or Walt, or Chris… Maybe… I knew I liked when Ernie came around, but it just wasn't the same as it was with the old guys. I could've sat there and analyzed the hell out of the situation for the next ten hours and still never predict the outcome, so I……………………

………………………..clipped the smoke, grabbed the coat, and headed out the door.

Ernie dictated the directions.

—A few blocks over

—Made a right somewhere

—Ended up down a dead end; a little private street.

—Only house on the cul-de-sac.

It over looked the Great South Bay. Expensive cars piled up everywhere. I clenched my jaw so tightly I thought I might've cracked a molar.

What the fuck? I said, pointing to the obvious before us.

Ernie head-butted the dashboard repeatedly, saying, ten people. Ten people. Rugo said only ten people at the fucking most.

A bizarre storm of a situation and boredom and fear and fuck the thoughts that won't stop in my brain and feeling naked and stupid as the cold wind roared, whipping my cheeks, freezing the nose, lips, cracked, dry, swollen, stirring points of anxiety in his eyes, asking myself how to read him? How?

Well, we're here. I said, and climbed out.

A surge of adrenaline burned through my skin.

We walked up the ice covered steps and into a jam-packed house. Every girl and guy had a can of beer and a smoke. All the girls were pretty and wouldn't look at me. Very modely. Very pursed lips and sucked-in cheeks. Acted poised and superior. They wore pleated skirts and chinos. The guys were handsome, tall, built. Polished loafers. Clean sneakers. Wrist watches. Collared shirts with buttons. They brushed their teeth and slicked their hair back or to the side. Pants ironed and cuffed at the bottoms. And there I was in my torn shirt, my one pair of baggy, frayed jeans, my torn-up Airwalks, and shaggy hair that hadn't been cut in months. Knowing you don't belong is hard; everyone making you feel like you don't belong is the hardest. If I could've made myself invisible, I would have. This is why I like being alone, away from the drama and bullshit gossip, away from all the people who do nothing but act as dead weight around your neck and sink you way low to the bottom. So, the loneliness doesn't seem so lonely after all.

Ernie kept bitching about Rugo but I didn't listen. I was trying to find some kind of redeeming quality about these people and enjoy myself, but it just wasn't happening.

Ernie grabbed some random girl who looked like a poodle.

Hey, ya seen Rugo?

Nope. Hey, Sally! Ya seen Rugo?!

This Sally person popped out of the crowd.

Yeah! He's in the mudroom! Wayyy in the back... that'a way!

And we followed her finger, that'a way.

What the fuck is a *mudroom* and why are they there? I thought to myself.

—Ernie took off through the crowd

—I followed

—Shoulders, arms bumping

—Hair-sprayed hair in my mouth

—The mudroom filled with pot smoke. Thick clouds of it.

—Dark and cold. I could see no faces, only shadowed shapes. The door kept opening then closing, and someone new would come in, or leave.

Ernie was... someplace in the blackness. Heard his voice quibbling with another guy, possibly this Rugo person, but I wasn't sure.

Then, a voice from the darkness spoke to me:

Whassup wit'm clothes? They make you tough or sumptin?

I went to answer, then...

—A punch between the shoulder blades knocked the breath out of me. As I turned around, someone opened the door, light from the party spilled in on Glen Davis, hands in pockets, and another pair of fists through the opening of his arms, doing the punching for him. Fucking pussy.

Felt the fists on the back of my head, then the cold ground under my knees...legs shaking, hands cramping from holding them so tight.

Aw, you're not hurt, are ya? asked Glen. C'monnnnnnnnnnn... ya ain't hurt. Get up.

I couldn't answer. Every time I breathed, something pulled from deep inside the back like my lungs were going to collapse. Every breath... Every breath the pain shot up the spine.

I thought he was a lesbian when I first saw 'em, a laughing voice said.

The fists took another swing. I tried swatting it out of the way but I got nailed on the forearm and the muscle clumped into a tiny ball.

A kick from the other side

And another

And a kick to my shins—

They ROARED with laughter

And Ernie told them to knock it off. They faked feeling bad about it and said:

We're just playin around. C'mon. We got nuttin against ya, swear it. Cross my heart.

He patted me on the sore spot of my back and I felt another hand rub my shoulders.

We're just a lil high is all. No big deal, man. We'll stop.

I tried catching my breath. I dug my knuckles into the muscle to rub out the pain. Then fists on the back, and Glen pummeled me over the head with his fists and I kept shoving him/them away, fists from all directions, dragging my knees over the cold ground, skinning the knee caps, burning/stinging, tried to get up and was punched on the jaw, bounced off the wall and fell to the floor then staggered in darkness and smoke and fists punching out of the smoke, then retracting and—

A   LOUD   FEMALE
AAAAAAAAAAAAAAAAAAAAAAAAAAAAAAAAAAAAAAAAAH

From the other room. Everyone pushed passed me; I squeezed in between legs, crawling out the way of the light the way out of the smoke and out of the blackness to the light.

NO ONE MOVED

SOME CRYING GIRL LOOKING OUT THE WINDOW

SOME CRYING GIRL, HER FACE HIDDEN IN HER HAND

MY CHEEKS SWOLLEN, BUMPS KNOTTED UP THE SPINE

I GOT CLOSER

SHE DROPPED HER HANDS AND REFLECTED IN THE WINDOW SHE SAW MY

EYES AND MUTTERED I'M SORRY I'M SORRY I'M SORRY SORRYYYYY

SHANNON.

I DON'T UNDERSTAND—

A cold wave hit me on the back and the blood in my body froze.

By the time I got outside and reached the last step—

MY BLUE CAR, BLUE OF THE CAR FADED, RUSTED, FLAT-TENED TIRES, BUSTED WINDOWS AND CRACKED SPIDER-WEBBED WINDSHIELD AND I HAVE NO MONEY I HEARD MA'S VOICE CRYING INSIDE MY HEAD I HAVE NO MONEY.

I faced the house and SCREAMED and SCREAMED so hard I ran out of breath. KILL ME KILL ME INSTEAD WHY DONTCHA? WHY DONTCHA?

The faces in the windows ugly drawn faces I could've killed I would've shot and bloodied their eyes and blown out brains splashing and splashing and—

GOD

GOD

GOD

FUCK YOU GOD YOU SUCK COCK

YOU LAIR AND ALL YOU'RE WORTH
AND VIOLENCE ALWAYS WINS
MIND WENT PITCH DARK!!!!!!!!!!!!
I don't remember getting in my car, or driving AND—

BACK HOME, THE NEXT MORNING...
Phone! yelled Ma pounding away at the door.
I stuck out my hand. It was A HEADACHE morning. A crumby ugly grey morning. She placed the phone in my hand. And there was no voice. Just breathing. Diversion. Then—
Seems like ya got some enemies. Whole lot'a people don't like ya. And neither do I.
SAY ANOTHER WORD TA ME... I FUCKIN DARE YA—
Then IT said:
If nobody liked me... and fucked up my car... and thought I was *ugly*, I'd probably wanta kill my—
YOU DO IT FOR ME FAGGAT. I FUCKIN DARE YA—
A dial tone like a bronze gong.
MRS. DEATH WAS THERE I COULD FEEL HER AND WANTED TA FUCK HER AND FEEL HER COLD BREATH BLOW ON MY NECK AND HAIRS WILL RISE AND BECOME ONE WITH AIR AND EARTH AND ALL—

THE NEXT DAY, THE NUMB WALK TO SCHOOL, THROUGH THE ICED GROUND AND SLUSHY BROWN SCUMMY SNOW AND WALKED AND
THE CANNIBAL EYES.
THE DAY LIKE A DREAM WHERE YOU'RE FLOATING THROUGH AND THE SCENERY IS THERE BUT YOU CAN'T FULLY REMEMBER IT AND THERE'S ALL SORTS OF CHAR-ACTERS ANIMATING IN AND OUT AND SOME HAVE JUMBLED UP FACES OF DIFFERENT PEOPLE YOU KNOW OR DO NOT KNOW AND WHEN YOU WAKE UP YOU GET THIS

FEELING THE DREAM WAS REAL LIFE AND THE LIFE
YOU'RE WAKING UP IN IS REALLY THE DREAM.
    really the dream.................
    ....THE NIGHTMARE

I STAYED IN THE LIBRARY WAY IN THE BACK. PLENTY OF
SUN THERE.
    PEACE. SUN. THE 8TH PERIOD BELL—
    THE WALK DOWN THROUGH THE GYM
    THE CROWD THAT FOLLOWED
    THE COACH STANDING CENTER OF THE GYM
    THE GUYS AROUND HIM
    THE SNEERS
    DIRTY SCABBED FACES
    THEY OWE ME THEY OWE ME I SAID
    THEY KILLED MY CAR AND THEY OWE ME
    AND THE COACH ASKED IF IT WAS TRUE
    SUCKIT -- IT'S TRUE
    I DARE YA TA SAY WHAT YA SAID ON THE PHONE TA ME
I DARE YA TELL ME TA KILL MYSELF YA FUCKIN FAGGAT I
DARE YA COME ON TELL ME TO DIE GIVE IT TO ME LIKE I
GAVE IT TA YA MUTHA LAST NIGHT O MRS. DAVIS TOOK IT
IN HER ASS WITH A BARBWIRE DILDO AND SHE SHOULDA
SHOVED YA BACK UP HER CUNT AFTA SHE HAD YA, YA
FUCKIN FAGGAT--

THEY WENT AT ME AND THE CROWD GOT IN THE WAY
SQUEEZING IN BETWEEN THE LEGS AGAIN I TORE AT
THEM AND GRABBED HIM, I GOT HIM AND BIT DOWN THE
SIDE OF HIS FACE AND TORE A PIECE OFF AND FELT THE
BLOOD AND SKIN BETWEEN MY TEETH—

———

THEY SENT ME HOME. THE POLICE WERE THERE AND I
WAS HOME AND MA CRIED AND DAD EVEN CRIED AND
MAGGIE HID AND I WENT TO MY ROOM AND CRIED/DIED
TO JESUS ON THE GOLD CROSS.
I WANTED TO GIVE MYSELF TO HIM HAND MYSELF OVER
GENTLY, GENTLY SLOWLY.

O GOD I'M FUCKED FOR BELIEVING IN YOU AND
RIDICULED FOR WHAT I BELIEVE IN OR I'M FUCKED FOR
NOT BELIEVING IN YOU THEN THE GUILT WILL HAUNT ME
UNTIL I DIE AND FIND OUT THE TRUTH
O GREAT CREATOR OF BEING I AM READY FOR A
TRUTH—
SMASHED TWO FISTS TO MY EYES TILL THEY WERE
BLOODIED
TILL I COULD ONLY SEE A FRACTION OF LIGHT
TWISTED THE SKIN ON THE SIDES OF MY THIGHS
TWISTED AND PULLED AND PICKED AT IT
THE TINY LITTLE HAIRS
ONE BY ONE
PICKED THEM OFF
AT THE ROOT
more PAIN no MORE
IT SPARKLED IN THE CORNER OF THE GARAGE AND IT
WAS MAGGIE'S
IT CALLED FOR ME, SPARKLING THERE LIKE A KING'S
RANSOM
I WALKED DOWN TO THE BEACH
THE JUMPING ROPE, THE SPARKING JUMPING ROPE
SPARKING BITS OF LIGHT AROUND MY NECK AND OVER
THE BOUGH—
THE NOOSE SLIPPED AND I FELL INTO A PATCH OF
LEAVES AND LAID THERE STARING AT THE SKY THROUGH
THE BOUGHS AND THOUGHT THE SUN LOOKED FAMILIAR

THE WAY IT SHONE THROUGH THE TREES AND SCIN-
TILLATED!!
I CRIED
PAIN IN MY THROAT
CREASES IN ARMS STUNG LIKE MOSQUITO BITES
THEN ALL OVER THE TUMMY
INFLAMED WITH STINGING BITES OF ITCHING PAIN
THE WELTS SWELLED
I RAN, STUMBLED INTO THE STREET AND—
MIND WENT PITCH DARK...

———

The door was flung open. Light jumped out through the door, escaping from the hospital. I wanted to go with it, but instead I was wheeled through a series of corridors then placed against the wall. Nurses and doctors rushed around everywhere, asking questions, yelling. Then a pinch on my thigh. I peeked down and saw a nurse retracting a needle. Within seconds I could breathe again and my chest relaxed and the pain assuaged. All the itchiness resolved.

There was a fat kid next to me throwing-up in a metal basin. Must've been around my age. His face had welts and cuts all over it. His mother cried, telling the nurses some kids jumped him at school and bashed his head against the locker. I almost cried listening to her because I know how he felt.

Mom, Dad, and Maggie came. Dad said nothing. Just pulled up an orange tin chair and read a magazine. Ma rubbed my head and told me I was going to be okay. Maggie stood there and stared at the fat kid, the loud groaning vomiting fits amplified from the metal basin.

Why is he doing that? Maggie asked Mom.

Maggie asked the same question again.

Ma didn't answer, she was too busy analyzing the bag of fluid going into my arm, and asking every nurse who walked by, what was in the bag. She demanded to know because she was the Mother.

Then Maggie yelled, *why does he keep doing that?!*

Shut up, I don't know what's wrong with the fat kid! said Ma.

I lay there, pretending none of this was happening, and they weren't my family.

After another hour or so, I was discharged and given a pred-nisone pack to take home. It was mandatory I finished the entire thing to ensure the hives do not return.

Ma ran a hand over my hair and said she loved me.

————

I finished the last two months of school at home. I visited Chris a couple of times. We watched Happy Days and ate pancakes and scrambled eggs. He laughed his laugh, and although he'll never be the Chris I used to know, he seemed happy and I was fine with that.

Ernie's parents bought him a brand new car that summer. A black Trans Am. I thought it was wonderful. Too bad I never saw the inside of it. I didn't attend the graduation ceremony and I got my diploma in the mail. Ma and Dad took me to a seafood restaurant on the Bay for a surprise graduation party. It was small. Nana, Pop, Aunt Lydia, Grandma and Aunt Jan came.

Gram sat next to me and handed over a thin gold necklace with a saint at the end of it. I thought it was wonderful even though I don't believe in God. I took the saint and placed it around my neck. I promised I would never take it off. She smiled and kissed my face.

Dad told funny stories about his painting adventures with Timmy and he finally smiled. Ma got drunk on Kahlua and milk and Maggie ate all the popcorn shrimp. Me and Aunt Jan had a spitball fight and laughed until our stomachs hurt. Everyone around us must've thought we were nuts, but I was fine with that, because it's the truth.

That was all; that was it. Nothing else to that very day even came close.

———

The remainder of the summer moved slowly, and I moved slowly in its movements.

I applied to a couple of city schools and got into all of them, but I chose Hunter University. It was in a pretty area, and I wanted to be around pretty things.

Towards the end of August, Ma woke me up on the hammock and handed me the portable. I heard a voice I didn't think I'd hear from again. Stanley just started talking. I can't remember what about exactly, but I remember his voice and it was filled with excitement. He told me to *come on down,* Walter and Rayanne were there and they rented some horrors they thought I'd like. He acted as though nothing ever happened. And maybe nothing really did. I smiled and looked up at the trees and the rays of light scintillated through the wavy boughs. I felt it's warmth in the air and all around me. I could hear the birds talking back and forth to each other while the sun continued to fill my body right through the heart—

TO BE YOUNG...

SEGUE #1

CHAPTER 2
ALL HALLOWS EVE

KNOCK

KNOCK

KNOCK

DING DING

I got this one! yelled Walter and ran to the front porch and grabbed a handful of candy from the can at the door and dropped the pieces into the bags of Darth Vader and the Ghost Busters.

THANK YOU!

And plates of hot food lay everywhere: lasagna, fried chicken, pizza, buffalo wings, chips, Doritos, popcorn, candy, bags and bags of candy, and a plastic garbage can filled with more candy at the front door which read TRICK R TREAT in black marker across the front.

DON'T FEED THE DOG CHOCOLATE JONATHAN! screamed Momma.

Jonathan stuffed the pieces in his mouth instead and told her he'd never do such a thing, and Stanley pumped the volume and chainsaws and screams ripped through the air and Walter turned away and Jonathan leapt off the couch and kissed Momma on the cheek for being such a great Mom and cooking them all that food and she swatted him away with the spatula and said

Get away! Get away! You're the reason why I got this hole in the roof ya little bastard! I'm still pissed about that!

And the kids roared with laughter.

Rocky sat at their feet while they watched horror movies, smoked their smokes, and talked their gossip about the neighborhood kids and

LAUGHED and

LAUGHED some more

KNOCK

KNOCK

KNOCK

DING DING

A couple of neighborhood kids on the stoop; their pillowcases wide and waiting. Bill was the clown, Jordan the pirate, and Shelly had on all black. She made sure she kept her head down. Whatta ya say? asked Jonathan.

They looked at him, dumbly.

Ya ain't gettin shit unless ya say it.

He waited…

Trick or treat, mumbled Jordan and Billy. Jonathan threw them a few pieces of candy. Who are ya suppose'a be purdy girl? She lifted her head and brushed the plastered blonde curls off her brow. Her face streaked with black and white paint. Her mouth like a skeleton. She smiled. Her little upturned nose high in the air.

DEATH, she answered.

PART TWO
ATROPA BELLADONNA

JOHN 3:8 COMMENTARIES:

The wind blows where it wishes, and you hear its sound, but you do not know where it comes from or where it goes. So it is with everyone who is born of the Spirit.

CHAPTER 3
SWEET SIXTEEN!

SHELLY DESERVED THE BEST. At least, *she* thought she did. A Knights of Columbus Hall is what she got, but inside her mind it glittered like the Château de Chambord. They danced, spread out across the floor and smiled, yelled, and cheered. The moms came up and announced to everyone this is *our* song, and this is how *we* use'ta do it back in *our* day. They lined up and did the Hustle to Night Fever in perfect synchronicity. Shelly clapped, and stomped, smiled, laughed. All the kids moaned. Shelly could have any song she wanted, but she loved the old disco stuff from her mother's era. The kids moaned, made motions with their hands (man, get this shit off!) But the moms didn't listen to them.

SHADDUP YA LITTLE PRICKS!

They just kept on dancing… and they could *really* move. Some of the girls followed along. It looked fun. Why not? Glittering dresses, high heels, awkward and wobbly for the sixteen year old shufflers. But the moms showed them the way. Back two steps, CLAP. Forward two steps, CLAP. Roll the hands in a circle with your hips like this, and point to the moon. And the girls weren't half bad. They tried, learned something new. What did they care, the boys were acting like a bunch of hardasses, sitting at their tables, posturing, heckling the DJ. Especially Billy, with that malicious childlike smile, a stark contrast to his clear blue devil eyes. Billy ran a hand over his Kool-Aid hair and called out, Hey big T! Move them thighs, fatass! Theresa flipped him the bird and rolled her eyes. At five foot two, barely breaking a hundred pounds, she knew he took a cheap shot at her, then deepest fear of ending up like Mother: Also five foot two, but the bottom half of her curved out like a giant bell.

Shelly squeezed all she could out of her night.

Queen of the room.

Château de Chambord.

Queen of the night.

The little Queenie. A delicate fairy amongst a forest of trolls. All the gifts. All the cake. All the envelopes (from both sides of the family, friends, and the parents of friends). The hugs and cheek kisses, and the compliments of how gorgeous she is — preternaturally beautiful— and how she looked twenty, not sixteen.

OH THAT SHAPE

WILLYA LOOK ATTA?

A MARILYN MONROE

THAT FACE!

Shelly spun and twirled for them, cheeks pulsing to lips, really *eating* it up, showing off the white blinding glam, molded after a traditional wedding gown, lace frills, but much, much shorter. Daddy grabbed her waist and pulled her in for the father daughter dance and told her how it was like staring into her mother's eyes the first time he ever danced with her 17 years ago, back in '79. The Policeman's ball. Ditched his date for her, and that was that. Shelly heard this story a thousand times, but in that moment, something moved her about it; the way he told it. His voice softened and cracked just a bit, trailing off into a whisper at the end of each sentence. But you're even more beautiful and he brushed the blonde wisps off her forehead.

Yknow, I tellya Mother all the time, you're my only true love.

A lump clotted her throat. Her small, well-defined mouth and proud upturned nose began to twitch as her grey-blue eyes sparkled with tears. And Pale Blue Eyes lingered it's song on until…

THE VERY END

Even Billy watched without a thing to say—

After the Sweet Sixteen, that asshole Jordan picked them up. Shelly and Theresa hopped in the back and Billy got shotgun. They drove down to Cedar Beach and lit a small fire and Jordan drank from the bottle and passed it to Billy, who passed it to dancing Shelly. Dancing between her friends and the clapping waves, twisting snake trails with her feet in the sand. Her little voice singing over and over the words to her song, her personal and freeing song of abject teen idealism—

If I could make the world as pure
And strange as what I see
I'd put you in a mirror
I put in front of me
I put in front of me

Shelly's life spun like a centrifugal force around anxiolytics (Ativan, Xanax, or anything she could get from Jordan)…. and alcohol. Although alcohol wasn't as accessible as the pills, when ever it was there, she'd indulge until blackout. She wasn't the type to steal booze from her folks. She had great respect for them, especially her father, whom, if caught his eldest daughter lifting the hard stuff from the locked cabinet, would have surely nailed her to the wall like he did with the elaborate array of mounted animal heads that adorned his wood paneled smoking room as trophies. No, no, no, no, no, not Shelly. She left the stealing up to Billy. Well, because he was accessible and stealing was his art. Billy was always there like the beauty mark above her lip.

Billy was 13 the first time he got arrested. He got caught defacing the headstones at Mt. Sinai Cemetery. Nothing new. Just a coupla dumbass kids on Halloween being what they were: punks. But the cops who caught them wanted to make an example of them for the rest of the kids in the neighborhood, despite the fact that they were minors. They were arrested. Booked. And brought before a judge who found it difficult to retain his laughter as he made Billy promise to be a good boy and not deface public property or next time the punishment would be severe.

A few weeks later he stole a car. This time it was with Jordan, who was a year older. They'd walk the streets around 3, 4am. Jordan's dad was a locksmith and he carried his old man's slim Jim and worked it like a pro. They'd hit low-end cars, nothing that brought them too much attention. Busted up Cavaliers, Toyotas, Datsun's, old, beat up Brady Bunch station wagons and they'd drive them all around, pick up their friends for school, get high, and when the car ran out of gas, they'd leave it wherever they were. One of the cars, an '86 Honda, had a 9mm in the glove compartment. Jordan secreted it in his backpack and it wound up firing off in the boys room when he plopped it on the floor to take a piss. It blew a hole right through the bathroom stall door, missing Billy's head by a few inches. He shot off the bowl, face forward, pants around ankles. They were each caught, but Billy was released. Jordan was placed in a youth detention center for 2 years, and when released, he looked like a grown man at seventeen. Jordan was bigger and stronger than most kids his age and took great pride in his ability to fight. He showed Billy and Shelly a stick and poke tattoo he got on his wrist while serving time. It read in cursive:

THE WILD COWBOYS.

Some crew from the Bronx put me down, he said. Them fags started off fuckin wit me all the time and wouldn't let up, especially this one guy Jesse, and one day just freaked out and smashed my lunch tray on his forehead. Gave'm fifteen stitches there. Thought I'd get shanked after that. But they got ta know me and put me down with their crew.

And Billy wanted to be like *them*. And to become like *him*.

There was something about spending time in the detention

hall that he enjoyed. He'd go down to the pizzeria, where all the guys would be hanging out, playing video games and buying endless rounds of cokes, garlic knots, and large triangular slices with extra cheese, sitting there in wraparound booths, telling stories about the "Cowboys" while doing time. None of the kids could relate. They weren't from the nicest areas but still, none of the guys took their antics to the places Billy and Jordan did.

He told them about two guys who blew a kids head off while they were driving down the Belt Parkway. It was a part of a gang initiation. He bragged about knowing both of them while locked up. They killed a guy. And that was magic for him.

Yknow the guy AJ? The one you seen on TV fa firing the .45? That's my G. When we fought dem Baby Bloods he was movin through'm like dey was nuttin. He'd dropped'm like that. He was built to be in the system. He always said he didn't know how ta live any other way. And lookit what happened? He's out no mo then a year and he's right back in. But dis time, he's bein tried as an adult. Only way he knows how ta live. He's a straightup G.

Shelly rolled her eyes at the story, giggled, and pointed at Billy's earnest face. They were corny to her, but at least they weren't as corny as the preppies. The guys that did everything their parents told them to do. The clean guys who always combed their hair, wore buttoned shirts, upturned collars, pleated pants. The ones who walked a straight line and made friends with all the teachers. They made her stomach contract in violent spasmodic fits. The feeling went beyond a simple eye roll and sideways sneer of mockery. It was a complete and total rejection of, what she called, the *Normies*. A clean society of herded sheep.

Shelly got a kick out of teasing Billy too. She'd refuse his kisses, pushing his face away calling him a mutt, a poser, and that he wished he was Jordan. A true G and she'd bust out in hysterics, especially at the word, G. There was an uneasy symbiosis among them, but it somehow worked. They fed off the fire and tension, and mockery and pseudo worship, and followed the fire down dark roads until the flame was no more than a sparkler dim.

. . .

EARLY ONE SUMMER EVENING...

Jordan met them at Cedar Beach and brought a tiny bag of dope. It's like god's breath blowing in your ear, he told them. Get in the car. And they did. They drove through the twisting tree-lined streets of the hilly North Shore to a hidden spot at the end of the lowest point of a hill, overlooking the Long Island Sound. A small, ancient stone hut rests on the hill, partially obscured by an overgrowth of vines and trees. Inside the hut there are two cement benches, covered with ivy and moss.

COME IN

Jordan said to Shelly, pulling her by the hand. Billy was already inside, flickering his lighter like a strobe, burning his thumb while did it. They sat on the benches. Shelly's face tightened, as she suffered vertigo in the featureless, dark environment. Jordan took out the dope and boiled it up by holding the lighter under a metal spoon. As he sucked up the liquid with a syringe, he said—

Yknow this is where that witch use'ta sacrifice animals and shit, back in the 1600's or sumptin. She was like our age. Anyway, the townies found out about it and dragged'a outta her house one night and hung'a right over there on that tree. The one on the cliff. See?

Jordan smirked as Shelly squirmed. The fact he got a reaction, any reaction, curled the corners of his mouth which laced his eyes into two black slits.

They say if ya flash a light over there you'll see'a hanging onna rope, twisting in the wind—

Shelly kicked his shin, Alright knock it off tough guy. Stop distracting yourself.

Whatta ya scared, Shell?

I can give a fuck about ya stupid ghost story, *faggat*.

You callin me a faggat?

Ats what I said, fuckin showoff. Ya ain't got the balls.

Jordan distracted himself away from Shelly and ordered Billy to hold a light on his arm so he can find a vein.

Two morons. This guy's playin Mr. Spooky tryin ta shoot up in the pitch black. Real smart, ya fuck.

I did it a few times when I was lockedup. I know what I'm doin.

Jordan took a handkerchief and wrapped it around his bicep. He tapped the vein and lowered the dropper, probing for the thickest part of pulsing blue… Shelly would not break her gaze from the throbbing flesh. Billy held the light steady, and Jordan slipped the needle in and pressed down on the plunger. His jaw tightened before it relaxed.

Shelly popped up and looked out the square hut window

You guys are retarded. If the cops come—

A EUPHORIC SIGH interrupted Shelly's next thought. She peeked at Jordan. Billy still had the light shining stubbornly on Jordan's face as if he were a staged actor. His entire body slumped into a beautiful state of relaxation.

It's like god's breath blowing in your ear… Shelly repeated the phrase over in her mind. She thought of a warm sensation filling her chest and her nerves calming to the slow ease afterglow of an orgasm. Maybe nothing would frighten her, nor make her nervous. No more tense legs or cracking of the knuckles. Or grinding the jaw, or wanting to leap out of whatever car she was in because she simply could not take the claustrophobic panic, which set far and deep into her bones as if her entire body caved inward, and all that was inside flowed outward. Maybe it'd take away the sadness, instead of delaying it, like the Ativan. Nothing hurt more than the gnawing depression centered in her chest, making it impossible to rise at dawn and lift her head from the pillow that became her resting security of sanctity.

It's like god's breath blowing in your ear…

Jordan nodded; his head drooped down like a dying flower. Billy smacked his face to revive him, but Jordan didn't move nary a muscle.

He better not be dead, said Billy.

Willya take the needle outta his arm.

Billy winced, Ew, I ain't touchin that thing. It's got his fuckin blood on it!

Keep ya voice down, ya freak, whispered Shelly through gnashed teeth. Now, move.

She grabbed the flashlight from Billy's hand and shined it on the stuck needle. A dribble of blood rolled down his forearm. Shelly bit her bottom lip and slid the needle out. Jordan's eyes fluttered. He took a sudden, deep intake of breath. Billy gasped air from his nose and shot up.

Holy shit!

She ignored Billy and tapped Jordan a few times on the side of his face. The corner of his mouth lifted to a sleepy grin.

Billy moved closer and stared into his eyes, Man, I thought you were dead.

Your breath stinks, said Jordan. Fuck outta here.

He took the palm of his hand and pushed Billy's face away.

Shelly asked him how he felt and he said, Beautiful…like god's breath…

Without hesitation, she grabbed the opened baggie from between Jordan's legs, dipped a curled fingernail in, scooped out a bump and inhaled the entire amount up her nose. A sharp, burning zing shot upward to her brain. The bitter drip of vile medicinal death slid down the back of her tiny throat. And she heard her father's voice mixed with an unfamiliar voice, dropped down an octave—

My little fairy, her father's voice said.

WE'RE ALL JUST DEAD FAIRIES IN THE END, said the other.

You're my *only* true love, said her father.

Dream on, said the other.

Shelly lunged forward and threw up.

Billy backed away. His body absorbed by the penumbra of the hanging tree.

Jordan slumped to his right, almost collapsing off the bench. He caught himself just in time so he wouldn't tumble off and somehow remained in that position, balancing his body between the wall and ground, his head bobbing on the nod.

The claustrophobic darkness strangled her, absorbing the saliva until the entire mouth dried, leaving only a thick film of paste, increasing the panic, the fear of suffocating, the need for water and Billy ran back to the car and got a bottle of water and she calmed, and warmth flooded the chest, shoulders, up and down the back, the legs, calves, feet, toes. A surge through her bowels and up her cunt, throbbing there and pulsing. Billy ran a hand over the top of her arm, the tiny hairs stood on end, he ran a hand up and down the spine, rubbing the neck, soft circles at the base of the head and Shelly watched the hanging tree sway and bob in the breeze. Crows flapping, cawing, screaming. They moved swiftly in the shadows, some appeared larger, humanlike. They attacked the rotted witch-body, hanging, picking at the eyes and nose and pulling strands of hair from the scalp. Opossums scratching at the feet, nibbling the ankles, tearing away sheets of skin, gnawing into bone, the crunching, the hard bone crunching. Billy's hand rubbed up her thigh. She passively placed a hand on top of his and gazed over at him. A weak grin. His finger slid between her legs and pushed there. The warmth of her groin. The wetness.

Please don't, she said squeezing his hand, crushing the fingers at the knuckles, felt the wetness of her cunt smear on her palm. Billy pulled his hand back. He stopped. Hoisted her up and took her back to the car. Jordan was passed out behind the wheel, engine running, headlights on. Billy banged the window and he awoke and adjusted the seat and sat up. He grabbed the inside handle of the door and slammed it shut in Billy's face. They took off. A few sloppy turns and one blown traffic light.

WHATTA YA DOIN YA JERK YA GONNA KILL US, slurred Shelly.

Jordan finally stopped at an intersection. Shelly got out and staggered away and over two blocks and down the long, long road of South Avenue. She thought about Billy and his hand there. Pressing in. Something excited her about it. When she'd masturbate, his face would appear, she'd cum, then feel ashamed, not understanding the compulsive thought of him during climax. But she hated him any other time after that and pushed this image way down to the unconscious where she'll keep until next time—

She remembered very little of the walk home, and through her darkened house and remembered very little of getting under her covers only to rip them back off and dry-heave several more times, slumped over the wastebasket. She remembered very little of her dreams that were so unpleasant and unsettling she awoke every few hours until dawn crusted the overcast sky.

For the next few days, Shelly thought about heroin and replayed the night over in her head (or what she remembered). She thought about it until she saw Jordan again. It was in his basement, on the mattress, while Dad was at work unlocking the helplessly locked-out, that Shelly *used* again. Jordan snorted it this time. No needles, he told her. From the previous injections, his wound turned into a throbbing green mess and he ended up on antibiotics for two weeks. They played tapes, talked, *used*, fucked (for the first time). Not for him, but for her. And it was like splitting an atom (after the junk wore off, the pain worsened) shaking the bed, the rocking and squeaking, a silver crucifix over the bed, banging against the wall, her stomach muscles clenched and sore and SCREAMING AT HIM TO STOP and the blood. THE BLOOD. The smell of it and her cunt. The feline odor. But Jordan kept banging, groaning, and Shelly screaming, wrapping her legs tighter, then loosening them, her thighs giving out and it took weeks for her to feel pleasure until the gnawing urge ate away at her belly again, fucking up her sleep, and she walked a half mile to his house, chucked a few pebbles at his bedroom window—

WHATTA YA NUTS?

COME THROUGH, she said, throwing her hands up.

He snuck her in through the basement and they split a bag and passed out. She awoke to him pouncing on her, banging against the mattress, biting the neck, her nails tearing shards of skin off his shoulders and back, BANGING, BANGING, SCREAMING, GROANING, AND BANGING. Jordan covered her mouth with his hand and got deeper and harder and he pulled out and came all over chest and throat and she squeezed the head, pinching the hole, forcing a few drops out and they slept.

For the next six months Shelly and Jordan used every day. She borrowed or stole money from Dad, Mom, or really anybody that could spare a few bucks, and she made up all kinds of excuses: clothes, new shoes, makeup, the pizzeria, the mall.

YA GOIN THROUGH ALL OUR MONEY, SHELL! I DON'T HAVE ANYTHING FOR YA. I'M CALLIN AUNT MARY AND ASKIN'A IF SHE NEEDS A SITTA FA DARYL. THIS IS GETTIN RIDICULOUS.

I AIN'T BABYSITTIN DARYL! THAT KIDS A RETARD!

TOO BAD. AND DON'T CALL YA NEPHEW A RETARD!

Mother called Aunt Mary and told her she could save her some money with daycare by having Shelly babysit for $25 a day.

I AIN'T GOIN SEVEN DAYS A WEEK! I'LL FUCKIN HANG MYSELF!

OH, SHELLY, KNOCK IT OFF YA BRAT! WE AIN'T GIVIN YA NO MORE MONEY, SO IF YA DON'T TAKE THE JOB YA AIN'T GOT SHIT! THAT'S THAT.

Shelly started babysitting Friday night. Before Aunt Mary left for the overnight she gave her instructions:

Kid goes ta bed at 9, no lata. And he knows this, so don't let'm pull any shit withya. Help yaself ta whatever's in the fridge and there's snacks in the top cupboard over the microwave, like ring dings, yodels and shit like that.

Hey, Aunt Mare… how old ya gotta be ta work in one'a those group homes?

Eighteen. Why? Ya wanta clean piss and shit 10 hours a day?

I'd work the overnights like you—

Plenty'a accidents happen durn the overnight sweetie.

Aunt Mary left and she was alone and the minute her ass hit the couch Daryl started in, laying on her lap, playing the itsy-bitsy spider crawling up her chest, copping a feel, and Shelly smacked him on the head and told him to get the hell off and watch TV and shaddup but he wouldn't and of course he started crying. So Shelly fed him a yodel and milk and put on a Charlie Brown tape, and the kid knocked out, and the urge hit her guts again, so she called Jordan and told him, but he's dried up till Sunday and—

I CAN'T WAIT TILL SUNDAY!

WELL, YOU'LL HAFTA.

WHO DOYA GET FROM? GIMME HIS BEEPER.

I AIN'T GIVIN YA HIS BEEPER. HE'S IN THE BRONX ANYWAY.

I DON'T FEEL GOOD, C'MON!

ME NEITHER.

I'LL HAVE $25 BY THE MORNIN AND I'LL PAY AND WE'LL SPLIT A BAG.

OKAY. MEET ME AT THE BASEMENT.

Her stomach shook with excitement and morning couldn't come soon enough.

They split a bag first thing Sunday morning and Shelly nodded and then Jordan and the winter sun rose and the beams came through the basement windows and warmed Shelly's eyes and she lifted her head and the burning in her stomach swished and she spat up a small amount of vomit, then heaved again but nothing but froth and out the window the world looked different to her. She moved her pants and underwear down and slid her hand down and rubbed over her clit and felt the warmth and wetness and stuck her fingers in there and with her other hand grabbed Jordan's thigh, moving up, and rubbed faster and harder and the sun brightened stubbornly across her eyes and shutting them did nothing, the dull pulse of the light burned a throbbing pain behind her sockets as her clit swelled full with blood and she slid her hand down Jordan's pants, rolled over and pulled out his cock, placed her mouth over and felt the soft warmth and sucked, keeping his cock in her mouth but it wouldn't get hard. Jordan moved, and clenched his legs together as the sun beat down on the side of her face as she bobbed and it grew and she put his hand on the back of her head and she went on with it until the pulse thrusted from his groin and filled her mouth with semen. She swallowed some then dribbled the rest back out, watching it slide down the shaft in a thick puddle.

THREE MONTHS LATER...

Her family began to worry. Especially Theresa.

Why are ya always sick? Whats'a matta?

And Shelly would often blow her off, condescending to allow her to ask any invasive questions. But there were obvious physical signs of decay no one could ignore. Her skin was yellowing. Dark bags under the eyes, sagging the skin low. Rarely would anyone see her eat. The school truancy letters piled up under her bed and later were burned (she didn't want anyone seeing those letters in the trash can, especially Mother, who had the compulsion to always inspect the garbage before bringing it to the curb). Mother hadn't seen a report card since December, and it was April. Graduation was two months away. The worry had set in. It was everywhere. In Mother's's eyes, in her smile, too heavy to show any teeth. In dad's face, when the worries from his job (the suicides — brains splattered across walls, hangings, unidentified, decomposing bodies found in the woods), those worries were supposed to lift and give him some ease as he'd sink down in his favorite recliner in the smoking room only worsened. His daughter, when she was home, looked less and less like his daughter and more like a person who was in the terminal stages of some irreversible wasting disease. Theresa finally broke her silence and told her folks kids around school were saying Shelly is hooked on dope and hung out with this disgusting lowlife by the name of Jordan. An eighteen year old drug dealer.

Shelly knew she was killing more than just herself, but her family too. As she awaited her parents on her personal proscenium in the dope drama, she thought of running away… only, she was too weak to get out of bed because she hadn't eaten in days, and, too dope sick because she was too weak to get out of bed and score some.

There was no fight when dad approached her laid out on the bed like a half-eaten corpse. He approached her as if he already knew, the same way he did it at work, when interrogating a convict.

How long ya been usin? Huh?

Shelly lay there, writhing, waving him off, then clutching her belly which caused her body to convulse and spasm.

Look, we know *everything*.

There's nothin ta know, she muttered—

Then dry-heaved. Little bits of froth and foam oozed from the corners of her mouth.Without saying another word, her father lifted her from the bed and motioned for Mother to follow. They drove her to Mt. Sinai hospital and wheeled her into the emergency room, where she was treated for malnutrition and administered the addiction-treating medication, methadone. As she regained her strength, Shelly threw a tantrum and SCREAMED and CRIED and banged her arms against the metal arm rests of the hospital bed and SCREAMED—

WHY DID YA HAVE ME YA MISERABLE CUNT?! WHY THE FUCK DIDYA EVEN HAVE ME?! FUCKYOU FUCKYOU FUCKYOU FUCKYOU FUCKYOU YA CUNT YA FUCKIN WHORE KILL ME KILL ME I HATE YOU SO FUCKIN MUCH FA HAVIN ME

She ripped the needle out of her arm and the nurses ran over and held her down and a male nurse administered Ativan to calm her and soon enough she fell limp. The hospital personnel wheeled her to the CPEP unit of the psychiatric department.

The next morning Shelly saw a social worker from the psychiatric wing who assisted her in finding an outpatient clinic close to her home.

GREAT. NOW CAN YA GET ME THE FUCK OUTTA HERE? I'M ABOUT TA EAT MY HEAD.

The social worker signed the discharge papers and mumbled how the place is packed and how they had nowhere to keep her anyway. He sent her home with a few addiction pamphlets and mental health pamphlets delineating symptoms of depression and anxiety and a number to call if she felt suicidal.

Mother brought her favorite afghan and wrapped it around Shelly and drove her home. She began addiction counseling the very next day. Mother waited in the parking lot while Shelly waited in the clinic waiting room. The cold tin chair bothered her. So did the people who surrounded her. Smelly, fat stomachs hanging over belts, yellow teeth, missing teeth, long greasy hair, Hispanic children yelling and screaming and running around and black children getting smacked on the head and yanked over by their mothers, cursing and pinching and slapping faces, and all the yelling intensified the growing nausea in Shelly's tummy. The rotted stench from the man who sat next to her. He scratched his crotch then smelled his finger and—

MICHELLE O'CONNOR…

O'CONNOR?

MICHELLE O'CONNOR?

SHELLY. No one calls me that, she said.

The intern apologized and took her to an office and closed the door.

I'm Melissa and I'll be doing your intake, today. How are you?

Shitty. How old are you?

Twenty.

You look familiar. Where'd ya go ta school?

Mt. Sinai.

Yah, ya look like a rich girl.

Melissa neatened the intake packet, re-arranged a few pages, and then grabbed a pen.

Date of birth?

May 13th, seventy-eight.

Ah gotta birthday coming up, I see.

Shelly nodded.

Social Security?

064-11-XXXX

Address?

Don't you guys have all this shit from the hospital?

We do intake with all new clients, said Melissa softly.

45 South Avenue, Patchogue NY, 11772.

You go to Buffalo?

Shelly nodded.

You know Brianna Cicchetti? She's a senior?

Big mouthy spoiled Italian girl. I know'a.

That's my cousin.

Shelly bit her lip and apologized.

No, its okay. It's the truth, said Melissa tittering softly.

Drug and Alcohol history?

Would drink sometimes.

About how old you'd start?

I dunno… round thirteen, fourteen I guess.

Drug addiction?

Little over a year. Started usin round last summer.

Drug?

What?

What. Drug.

Shelly leaned forward and said—*Dope.*

Melissa adjusted herself, crossed legs, shuffled papers…

Mental health history? Under any Psychiatric care?

Anxiety and depression. And no, just my GP.

Taking any medication for it?

She had me on Buspar but it didn't do shit. Then she switched me to Ativan and Paxil but not no more.

How'd it work for you?

It was okay. But I was tired all the time so I got off.

Shelly looked down her torn up combat boots, then looked to Melissa's feet in open-toe dress shoes. The pedicure. Light pink. Pretty. Her hands— long lacquered nails to match the toes.

Three goals you'd like to work on for the next few months?

Shelly sighed and rolled her eyes.

I know, but its corny, but it's part of the whole thing.

Well, I'd like to get a car. Does that count?

It does. Do you have your license yet?

Just my permit. I passed the written test though.

Ok, getting your license can be another goal. I need *one* more.

Shelly continued to stare at Melissa's feet, wondering what hers would look like in those same shoes with her toes painted the same way.

How about coming to treatment every week for the last goal?

Shelly thought it over, her eyes searching about the room, the open window, the overcast skies, the hanging plants, the motivational quotes tacked to a pegboard, Melissa's pleated skirt, her long, tea-colored hair, her makeup, the simple prettiness of her face, and finally said okay. And then she smiled.

Great, said Melissa, writing it down.

I'm gonna take you to Maryanne now. She's gonna be your counselor.

She escorted Shelly to the back of the building. Knocked on a door. The door opened. She handed Maryanne the intake form.

Okay, it was nice meeting you Shelly, said Melissa, smiling, and walked off.

Maryanne welcomed her in and Shelly sat on a nice sofa and Maryanne closed the door and…

Can ya keep it open, please? asked Shelly.

Of course I can, and Maryanne smiled a bright smile and walked across the room and pulled up a chair.

Shelly sucked on a finger and looked at the many paintings and framed photos of crows hung on the wood paneled walls.

I like birds, she said. But not crows. They kinda scare me.

Ah, they're very beautiful to me, said Maryanne. What scares you about them?

I dunno, she giggled.

Maryanne flipped through the intake papers.

How's Buffalo treating ya?

It's the pits. Hate it. My mother's having me home schooled for a while cos of all this stuff.

Good Mother.

She's okay.

Maryanne smiled again and reached back and set the papers aside on her desk.

They said I hafta take this stuff called methadone but I don't wanta be on anything and I don't wanta do that stuff again, so.

Well, that's good. I am extremely happy to hear that, but committing to a methadone treatment program for at least a year will likely change your life for the better and help you commit to staying clean. The first two weeks are crucial. You're going to have to come here every day to get your dose—

And Shelly phased out and a tear dribbled down one side of her face and she took her bottom lip into her mouth because she didn't want to come back this filthy clinic every day but it was something she had to do and she knew it. Her chest broke apart and the rawness of the moment finally sank in and her guts twisted in unrelenting anguish, her fingers pinching the sides of her thigh, the grinding jaw, the cracking knuckles, the bitten cuticles, the birds the birds

THE CROWS

FLAPPING

BITING

SCREAMING, MOANING

PICKING AT THE EYES

TEARING SHEETS OF SKIN FROM HER ABDOMEN

The stinging pain the searing slices the tiny cries and throat narrowing, collapsing, the stomach squeezing the bile up to the mouth, the bitter taste on the tongue—

EARLY MORNING— CLINIC.

One nurse served each person who came to this place of crumbling plaster and dark stairwells. More men than women, some dressed well and many not, lined up for the orange-colored concoction of methadone hydrochloride and Tang. In a ritual of relief, they gulped "the medication" in child-sized plastic cups. Shelly took the cup and downed it. She winced and walked out.

BACK AT HOME...

Mother brought Shelly her school work and she remained in her bedroom. All three meals, which were only half eaten, were brought up to her bedside, like a little Queenie.

Each day around noon— bored by the re-runs of old 70's and 80's sitcoms— she'd complete her ritualistic masturbation. She thought of nothing at all. She did it for the pure pleasure. The release. And each time she'd get a little closer to climax, she'd stop and delay the orgasm. Building and building, all the blood rushing to the pelvis and clit, swelling, and pulsing. She'd continue until the area was raw and throbbing. The soreness between her legs gave her a dull, pleasant ache. Then finally, almost crying at the spontaneous release of it, she'd clutch her neck with her free hand, and squeeze... and squeeze... and squeeze to the point of asphyxia. Until her lips were a violet-mauve, cold and pursed. She'd rest in that dark pleasure, the aftermath, the fluids still dripping out of her, creating a glossy spill covering the sheets. The nerves calming to rest, lulling the heart and breath in one rhythmic cycle. Falling into a blissful repose.

YOU'RE GOIN TA YOUR GRADUATION CEREMONY! AUNT MARY BOUGHT A CAMERA AND EVERYTHING! I

DIDN'T GO TA MINE AND I REGRET THAT SHIT EVERY GODDAMN DAY. YOU'RE GOIN TA YOURS! THAT'S FREG-GIN IT!

YOU GIVE ME NO FUCKIN CHOICE? YOU'RE A LOON! GO AWAY.

MID-JUNE...

Shelly returned to school to practice the moving-up ceremony. She did well enough on all the take-home assignments, and acquired the necessary credits to grant her a diploma. Everyone commented her on how good she looked and how thin she was. Even girls she never spoke to, teachers whom never acknowledged her, boys whose faces were unfamiliar yet filled with empathy, all expressed their concern. Even the ones who tormented and teased her, and grabbed at her—

HA! YA UGLY FREAK!

LOOK ATCHA?

WHO WANTS YA ANYWAY?

FREAK

FREAK

FREAKKKKKKKKKKKKKKKKKK

But she kept her composure and told them she was fine, and answered all the questions in a terse, delicate voice without revealing too much. The methadone still knocked her out, keeping the world hazy and old-movie-time hypnotic. The blonde waterfall curls that once framed her face, now fell in loose frayed strands, like knotted rope.

After snoozing through most of the graduation ceremony, Shelly took off her cap and gown and tossed them in the garbage. Underneath laid a second-hand dress, torn and splayed around the edges and along the bottom, which hung just above her scabbed knees.

Jordan wasn't there and Billy was just another face among the many. *Nobody* came to visit her. Billy called once while she was napping and she returned his call, the immediacy of the moment causing the tiny hairs on her arms and the back of her neck to stand, flushing her face a deep crimson— and she never thought the name "Billy," rolling off Mother's tongue would give such a sudden thrill. She called him back multiple times until finally his mother picked up and rudely told her Billy wasn't there and she'd appreciate it if she stopped calling. The cold slice of silence before the dial tone stuck with her and presented itself at various moments, when her mind was clear, or focusing on the beanbag in her room, where he'd sit each time he was over. There was maybe a few times she saw him during the last weeks of school, and as he exited the cafeteria he pushed right through her as if she were a ghost.

And Billy with his family, gesturing, smiling, laughing, posing for the camera, holding up his diploma. Shelly had enough of it. Enough of the phoniness. She lost her parents long ago, somewhere in the crowd, and wound up walking back to the car where she waited in the backseat.

A long, terrible car ride home. Dad asked questions but her eyes remained on the trees flowing along the wheeling roads and thought nothing more of it. Not the greenery or flashing rows of blue wild flowers offered her anything but a blur of color. Dad's voice was just a voice, and she nodded along with the bumps, and twists and turns—

HYPNOTIZED

HYPNOTIZED

A revolving splendor of hues.

EARLY MORNING— CLINIC.

Shelly lined up for the orange-colored concoction of methadone hydrochloride and Tang. In a ritual of relief, she gulped "the medication" in child-sized plastic cups. She winced and walked out.

. . .

She had to babysit that little brat. She wasn't sitting home doing nothing all summer. Every Tuesday and Thursday they settled on. Daryl. That little snot-nosed bastard. Shelly had the TV on, watching her music videos, singing along, and Daryl came by and smacked the OFF button on the TV.

TURN IT BACK ON YA LITTLE BRAT!

NO! PLAY WITH ME!

AFTER THIS VIDEO I WILL.

NO! NOW!

Shelly got up, moved Daryl out of the way, and turned the TV back on. Just as she turned away, What do you think Daryl did? He turned it back off.

PLAY WITH ME!

DARYL TURN IT BACK ON! I'M NOT GETTING UP AGAIN!

NO!

And he stood in front of the TV, hands folded.

I've had it ya little fuck, muttered Shelly.

HEY! YA SAID A BAD WORD! I'M TELLIN MA!

Shelly shoved him aside and he kicked her knee and.

ENOUGH!

Shelly pushed him down. Daryl lay there, confused, as if a grown person never put their hands on him before. He got up and stood, folding his hands behind his back.

Just let me watch my show please. If you behave, I will play with you later, promise.

Finger pressed ON button.

NO!

Daryl kicked her knee. Shelly, on impulse, closed her fist and drove it into Daryl's face. He fell back on butt, shocked. Too shocked to even cry.

Ow… my face hurts, Aunt Shelly.

Her eyes filled with water. She simply could not control it, or hold them back, or think them away like she did back in school when the kids were teasing her, hitting her, calling her crotch-rot, and fish skins, and freak.

Daryl, I'm so sorry, she said, crying. Are you okay? Are you—

Yeah… it's okay, he said, moving slowly away from her. His eyes swelling with fear.

I'm not gonna hurt you… I promise.

Shelly bent down and picked him up. Daryl, stiff, eyes agape, clutched to her, because his Mommy was working, and he missed her badly, even worse than before.

Shelly placed him down on his bed and lay beside him, hysterical crying. Daryl told her to please stop and it hurt his heart to see her so sad. He knew she didn't mean it.

It's okay, Aunt Shelly. Please stop cryin.

But she couldn't and she cried and cried and cried.

And Daryl slept.

During her weekly meeting with Maryann she suggested a search for a part-time job. When summer's over, maybe. Oh, I completed one'a my goals. I passed my road test.

And she said it while twirling her hair around her finger, slicing the cuticle, turning the tip purple.

TERRRIFFFIICCCCCCCCCCC! said Maryann, clapping.

Shelly had no real passion or aspirations, just diversion. Anything Maryann suggested, she'd consider, but later shrugged off. She liked Maryann, though. She liked her calm, gentle nature. Her long, bohemian summer dresses. And she *loved* that Maryann never put any sort of pressure on her when it came to making decisions, or answering questions. She'd tell stories about her life which related to various topics they'd discuss during session. One particular story repeated in Shelly's mind. The story about a baby crow Maryann found in her yard a few years back. It had an injured foot and she told in vivid detail how she nursed it back to health by creating a splint with a Popsicle stick and a gauze bandage. She didn't know the sex, but named it Harry, after her Grandfather. She kept Harry in a big iron cage in the sunroom until he got too big, and he'd stretch his wings the span of the cage, simulating flight. She'd talk to him every day, and he even picked up on a few simple words, like *hello, pretty bird, good morning*—the usual stuff. And towards the end of the year, he learned a phrase Maryann said every morning: *Oh Lord, pour the coffee!* And then one day, she let him go. She took Harry, cage and all, out to the backyard. The backyard he faced every season, while caged.

I slid the door open and out he flew straight up into a tree and released this big, beautiful, bellowing *CAWWWWWWW...* It was strange, because it seemed he didn't know what to do at first, but then as I watched'm up there—looking around, spreading his wings, flapping em in place—his instincts kicked in and he flew off into the sky.

Didya ever see'm again?

Impossible to tell, really. I do remember a few months later, in October I believe, I stayed home from work because with the flu— and that year was bad, bad, bad for the flu— '93—

Oh yeah, everyone was sick! I remember. They gave free flu shots in the gym and one girl had a seizure!

Oooo that's awful. Yeah, I'm not big on the flu vaccine, that's for sure. But anyway, all this racket woke me up from a dead sleep. All this *CAW, CAW, CAW!* So, I go run to the window and my trees are filled with crows. I *never* saw anything like it. All of'm screaming and flapping their wings. I remember thinking, well, this has never happened to me before, and I said to myself, *one of'm had to be Harry.* The only thing that made sense to me. So, I yelled up, HARRY! O HARRY POUR THE COFFEE! And I waited... and waited... and I heard nothing. Well, I got *a* response — more cawing and all that, but no words. I'd like to think he was there, though, among the group, somewhere. Maybe he lead'm back to my house—his house— his old house. Maybe they followed'm as he was flying back to say thank you, in his own way. But doncha know, they come back nearly every fall, and do the same damn thing. I keep a giant bird feeder out there, on the tree they all gather on, and sometimes I'll see a Robin, or a Cardinal, or maybe some Finch— one time I even saw a few Starlings, but the crows only come around during the fall. But they come back again, and again, and again…

Maryann noticed Shelly fixating on a specific crow painting. The abstract oil painting with thick textured streaks of black and different shades of blues and the colors melted and bubbled and the beak widened, opening WIDER—

Yknow, I have this reoccurrin dream where I'm layin in bed but I can't move, but I'm aware. I'm totally aware, but I'm frozen stiff. And this *thing* is off ta the side somewhere, and I can feel the presence of a large animal breathin. But I can't look at it.

Shelly looked to the crow painting and could see nothing but it's beady eyes, filled with hatred. She continued describing the nightmare while remaining transfixed on the crow:

All I hear is this breathin. This, like, deep, wolflike, demonic breathin. And I'm tryin *so* hard ta look outta the corner'a my eye, but all I can do is stay starin at the ceilin. And these claws start tearin away at my stomach and… down further, like, forcin itself inside me… And I can't look anywhere but up. And I feel the claws, I can *feel* the nails— pricking at my insides, tearing away bits and pieces at first, then pullin then yankin and twisting as he pulls harder and harder and it's like he's digging a fetus out of my guts because that's what he really wants and all I could do is lay there, stuck inside my head screamin, then I wake up screamin in real life, screamin Maaaa—

The oil colors from the crow painting bubbled and oozed droplets onto the floor, then small bits of feathered flesh, getting thicker and thicker, pouring liquid streams of blue turning black turning red—syrupy glops of blood, dark organ blood, raw chards of meat toppled out as the flapping and screaming and groaning climbed in octaves until finally reaching a sharp, penetrating sound;   one   long   thin   line:
EEEEEEEEEEEEEEEEEEEEEEEEEEEEEEEEEEEEEEEEEEEEEEEEEEEEEEEEEEEEEEEEEE

Shelly smashed her palms on each ear, opened her mouth to cry for help but gagged, then dry heaved, collapsing on her knees, violent, dry retches inflating her eyeballs and spasmodic jerks of her back, arching at the center like a cat stretching, her tongue hanging out, and she envisioned black gunk's of oil spewing from her mouth.

Maryann rushed over with a waste basket. Shelly retched again, but nothing came out.Shelly, I'm gonna get the nurse, okay? Okay honey?

Shelly broke down in hysterics, crying, panting, gagging, driving her fist into the side of her thigh, pounding out the frustration and torment.

Maryann grabbed the phone and dialed an extension—

Hi, Fran? Need ya in here fast. Full-blown panic-attack.

As she slammed the phone down, Fran rushed in with a plastic bag containing a syringe and a small glass canister filled with liquid.

Shelly saw this and her face contorted.

NO MORE FUCKIN DRUGS NO MORE FUCKIN DRUGS GET THE FUCK AWAY FROM ME!!!

Maryann got on her knees in front of Shelly and placed her hands on shoulders.

You remember what I taught you when this happens, right? Shelly look up at me, honey. Look up at me, please.

Maryann used a soothing, calm voice.

I have to make sure you're safe, okay? I called the nurse just in case. You don't have to take any medicine—

Shelly shook her head and placed both hands on Maryann's shoulders. Saliva and phlegm dribbled from her mouth and nose.

I don't wanna, I don't wanna, I don't wanna, she said, her body still heaving with hysterics.

Maryann motioned for Kleenex. Fran brought over the box on the desk and sat on the chair next to them. Handed Shelly a Kleenex.

I wanna be safe, I wanna be safe, I'm so sorry.

Maryann hugged her, rubbing between her delicate, winglike shoulderblades.

Shhhhhhshshshshshshshshshshhhhhhhhhhhhhhhhhhhhhhhhh-hhhhhh.

Shelly dug her face in Maryann's shoulder, motioned to Fran everything is going to be okay and that her assistance is no longer needed. Fran smiled, touched Maryann's shoulder, grabbed the paraphernalia and left.

Maryann walked Shelly outside to the parking lot. Shelly gasped. Slowed her breathing. Smiled as the clouds passed. Maryann sat her down on the curb, under the penumbra of a large tree. Wild flowers swayed against her arm. She touched the flowers and felt them wither beneath her hands. Above her head, the trees showed their first spots of brown.

I feel better, thank you for takin care'a me.

Honey, don't thank me. Okay?

Shelly nodded.

You're fine to drive?

She nodded again and got behind the wheel. Maryann smiled and waved.

Until 5 o'clock. That's it Shell! Come home right after session. Got me?

Mother's voice beat around in her head like a caged bird. But still, she decided to stop at the bookstore anyway. She figured, *fuck her* and went anyway and Billy crossed her mind first. One of her only friends. His face. Those heavy lidded eyes and puffy cheeks. He was a cutie when he was a kid. And that laugh. The wildly embarrassing guffaw and if he was really on a roll, it sounded more like a burst of hiccups, rising in octaves that wouldn't stop until she'd slap a hand over his big mouth. And then Jordan. The haze she remembered him in, diffident and subdued. The CRACK of virginity. The bleeding. The symbiotic nature of one upon another, floating in separate head trips, drifting like a couple of feathers downstream. And she gave him something he'll have forever and that saddened her, and the sadness dulled the heart and the tears oozed and dribbled from the sunken cheeks and plunked on the creases of her arms. He'd probably be happy to see her miserable, that piece of human burning garbage. But who cares? He's fucking gone now. Dumbass got caught stealing another car with possession of a firearm and a bundle of dope. Found himself in front of a judge who told him he could either go back upstate or join the Army. He chose the latter. Sorry Charlie. See ya later creep-o.

Thanks for nothing.

THANKS FOR NOTHING.

As she pulled into the parking lot of the bookstore, the lump reformed in her throat, the regurgitation, the stomach acid rising from the abdomen, the bitter taste on her tongue. Shelly remained seated, staring into the rearview mirror, watching her eyes shake and swell. She tightened her grip around the wheel and imagined her finger tips mashing her sisters face—that little fucking tattle-tale— mushing the skin away like melted wax.

The world would be a pleasant place to live if everyone would just mind their own goddamn business and stay the fuck outta mine!

The anger inflamed betokened of the mounting panic ready to spray a rainbow stream of upchuck. She needed a bathroom and to calm the fuck down. Breathe, like they told her.

BreathBreathBreathBreathBreathBreathBreathBreathBreath-BreathBreathBreath

The bullshit method never worked and made her more angry and feel less in control and she had nothing on her, nothing in the goddamn car!

NO BOTTLED WATER.

NO ANXIOLYTICS.

NO PLASTIC BAG TO VOMIT.

The same dumb-fuck panicky feeling from Maryann's office returned and what the fuck was she to do? There's no one around to help and the embarrassment of a full-blown attack in public had overtaken the ability to think rationally and calmly and

BATHROOM. NOW.

A quiet stall. The running water. The WATER!!! Her mouth—

cracked and pasted shut. Cellophane over the lips. A sock stuffed down the throat.

Shelly hurried inside the bookstore and followed the signs to the lavatory. The door closed behind her. SHUT. Banged five times. Closed. An elderly lady emerged from the stall. The click, tick, click of the latch and the door banged shut. Eight horrible times. BANG… BANG… BANG… Shelly darted into the stall and folded over the lid, slouched down and concealed her face in her hands, groaning, sobbing, and breathed. Breathed. Breathed in tiny asthmatic puffs, inflating the diaphragm and releasing. The breaths getting longer. All the slimy scum. All the worry. All the dirty, rotten guilt. Get it out. Every fucking bit.

Breath in::::::::::::::Let it come out::::::::::::: She screamed without a throat, without a tongue.Breath in::::::::::::::Let it come out::::::::::::: She let the mind go blank and let the eyes see nothing. After a few times, the urge to cry lessened. The nerves melted, unhinging the jaw, releasing the gnashed teeth. Deep into the relaxed state moments before the brain shuts off and drifts to unconsciousness.

Shelly got off the toilet, unlatched the stall door and walked over to the sink. She turned the handle counterclockwise, bent over, and sucked water from the faucet. *I want this to stop,* she screamed inside her head. *I want to turn off everything that hurts and won't stop thinking and feeling like this nightmare I once had and I thought I was awake but couldn't feel or see or hear anything and I couldn't even think I was just there floating in space and a dark growling cloud was at the ceiling spinning in a circle and I asked please god make all of it stop because it just doesn't ever stop and I wanna rip my guts out and tear the skin off my face pricking away every bit of skin until there's nothing left but skull. I hate myself I hate myself I hate hate hate hate hate hate hate hate stop please stop this please I don't wanna hurt anyone I'm afraid I might and I couldn't do it if it meant living with the reality that I hurt another person because I'm hurting I'd rather be fucking dead —*

Shelly sucked in her stomach and cooled her face with her hands, fanning the tiny beads of water into the skin, and pounded her fists on the edge of the sink then grabbed the porcelain, her wet fingers sliding off the edges, all the pressure going to the fingertips. The nail of her right index finger bent back and snapped, hanging by a bloody tag. Her hands trembled, vibrating, like motors under the skin, spasmed and pulsed. She examined the nail, loosely dangling on the top part of the nail-fold—

OH FUCK OH FUCK OH FUCK OH FUCK FUCKFUCKFUCK OWWWWWWWW!Bits of eyeliner rolled down each cheek. She bit her bottom lip, grabbed the hanging nail between the two fingers of her left hand, and yanked it off. The pop. A squeal like a stuck pig. A blob of blood formed then trickled down her finger. Shelly yanked out a hand full of paper towels from the dispenser and applied pressure to the index finger. She squeezed at the cuticle and the dull throb, the pressure, the pain curled the corners of her mouth upward. Slightly. Pressing harder, driving the thumb deeper into the cuticle, she peeled away the wet shards of brown paper. The bleeding had assuaged. Slightly.

She walked out of the bathroom and spotted a narrow aisle with no one around. She plopped down in the New Age section and pulled out a book on Palmistry. How the lines of your hand can tell the future. Nothing but bullshit. But still, there was something she found fascinating about it. The possibility that her lengthy success line could mean fame, sent shivers through her body. She always wanted to be a STAR.

A long haired young man sauntered by. They had similar boots. But there was something else that struck her. Something undefinable. She felt the urge, the same urge that tighten her stomach when she needed junk. The impulse. The magnetic pull. Led her over to him. Slouched facing the wall, reading. She studied him, the muscles of his back contract, the thickness of the neck, the slow movement of his hands. He turned to her slightly and Shelly turned down a different aisle. She grabbed a cookbook and tore off the bottom of a page, walked to the information desk, grabbed a pen and scribbled down her phone number. The blood from her index finger dripped on the first few letters of her name. She straightened her back, pushed out her chest, and walked toward him, watching his legs, the ass, bending, then straightening and she sauntered by, making eye contact, smiling coquettishly, sliding the paper in the side pocket of his jeans and the lightness in her stomach and chest and the anxiousness in her bowels. Finally, deciding that moment was the perfect time to depart, she sauntered out the front entrance, the blonde waterfall curls swaying. The QUEEN has left. Back to her throne. She knew nothing about him, not even his name, and she was fine with that and

Shelly drove home—FAST—smiling because her heart finally told her to do so... Because her heart was so wide with joy there was no way her body could contain the happiness ready to beat out of her and fly up into the trees like Harry and come back to the same tree with a hundred more friends to scream their guts out to a world who will never understand them, but hear the holy glory of the joy of being

A L I V E

EARLY MORNING— CLINIC.

Shelly lined up for the orange-colored concoction of methadone hydrochloride and Tang. In a ritual of relief, she gulped "the medication" in child-sized plastic cups. She winced and walked out.

FOR THE NEXT SEVEN DAYS...

Late night movies with Mother. Every day they'd pick a different genre, and rent a few movies they never saw. Mother put out nachos and cheese and salsa and cranked the AC so they could share their favorite leopard blanket. Mother had been on Xanax since the whole ordeal with Shelly and had been passing out on the couch. For WEEKS. Shelly wondered about Mother.

What did she think? What was she feeling? Did she still love Dad? Was I causing them to hate one another? Does she feel loved? By him? Did she ever truly feel loved by *him*? Could she love? She never said it to me… or him. Or Theresa. Do they still fuck? Does he find her ugly and her body less attractive? The last time they went to the beach together. As a family. Mother wore a sundress to hide the many folds, and the bloat. Her left leg (with all the broken veins) had swollen from diabetes. Like she had elephantiasis of the leg. Everything about her changed. Everything from the neck down, but—

Half way though horror night, Shelly snuggled closer and rested her head on Mother's chest. Smelled of fresh powder, lilac. Sniffed again. Kissed her collar bone. Raised her face and softly kissed her cheek and again, played with the tiny hairs on the back of the neck.

HOLD ME, demanded Shelly. Like when I was a baby.

Mother stiffened, eyes rounding, glued on the TV screen.

C'mon Momma, I wanta be your baby again.

Mother said nothing.

Shelly pecked her cheek and snaked her arm around the shoulder and pushed her face closer to her face and Mother's eyes would not leave the screen and Shelly turned 1/4 towards her face and gently pressed her lips against hers—

THE PHONE RANG

—and they did not break. Their lips remained together and as the phone RANG and RANG again, Shelly finally pulled away flicking her tongue around the edges of her lips.

She got up and sauntered across the room over to the end table and picked up the phone. The anticipation pounded through her chest.

HELLO… HELLO…? UH, HELLOOOOOOOOOOOOOO

Frustrated, she placed her fingers on the switch and a voice finally came through, calling her name in question.

Yes, this is Shelly.

Hey, remember me?

I don't know who "me" is.

Joey. Ya gave me your numba at the bookstore.

Shelly shifted and draped herself over the rocking chair. Anticipation rushed through her bowels.

And Mother threw her a vicious glance and the TV's volume increased and Shelly's heart accelerated but she controlled her speech and the pitch in her voice and took longer than usual to answer his questions of where she was from, and what school she attended, and how old she was. And she reversed some of the question back on him, even the questions she didn't answer.

SILENCE.

A battle of silence. Who would talk next and Shelly seemed to enjoy it. She seemed to relish the adroit sense of creating indirect chaos by simply not speaking.

As she cocked her head to the side she noticed Mother was gone. The blanket, a crumpled mess left on the sofa. The TV, still blaring. The end credits, rolling.

I hear ya sleeping…

Shelly inhaled, then exhaled into the receiver, letting the exhale fade to a humming: UMMMMMMMMMMM.

Wanta get some diner food? he asked.

Sure.

Shelly told him to meet at her at the end of South Avenue, the big park there; she'd be at the swing set. Around ten o'clock. She grabbed her JanSport bag, snuck out of the kitchen door, and walked a few blocks down to the beach/park. Sat on the swing. The creaking chains. The moonlight on the bay. The waves like claps of thunder. She kicked higher on the swing, her legs up, pointed toes; she felt she could kick the moon out of the sky.

The ROAR of an engine mixed with the waves and creaking swing and Shelly smiled. Her back faced the parking lot. She needn't turn around. The excitement rushed through her bowels. Joey walked up. Heavy boots on the sidewalk, stomping to sand, dragging, swing swimming, creaking and.

HIGHER! said Joey.

I'M KICKIN THE MOON!

Her smile opened. She pumped the legs out, thrusting her body up then pulling back while leaning forward.

GET ON! she screamed.

He did.

I WAS ABLE TA FLIP OFF THIS WHEN I WAS KID! she said.

BULLSHIT!

FUCK YOU!

NO WAY I BELIEVE YA!

WELL I CAN'T DO IT NOW!

Shelly kicked higher, and then leaned way back, cutting through the wind.

THAT'S COS YA STINK!

FUCK YOU!

LOSER! PUT THE MONEY WHERE YA MOUTH IS!

I SAID I COULD I DO IT WHEN I WAS YOUNGER, MORON! CHICKEN!

THAT'S IT! she said, laughing.

Shelly swung up high, flexed her legs, pointed the toes to the moon, released the chains and kicked her feet over her head—

TUMBLING

TUMBLING

TUMBLING

TUMBLING

And PLOPED right on her ass in a big hill of sand. She rolled over on her sand, laughing. Joey jumped off the swing and plopped beside her.

OHHHHHHHHHHH… NOW I GOT SAND IN MY PUSSY.

Yikes!

Yikes your ass. You don't have a pussy so ya don't know it feels, mister!

Maybe I do.

Shelly giggled and whipped a handful of sand at him. Joey covered his face and rolled away. Shelly rolled on top of him, placing her palms to his chest. The stare off. The silence.

Hey! I'm hungry!

Okay, let's go eat.

I want sausage…

Joey's eyes bulged.

…and pancakes!

She hopped off him and threw her hands up, fingertips to the stars—

…and French toast and scrambled eggs and bacon!

Show me where ya parked, said Shelly extending a hand. Joey grabbed her fingers and she yanked him out of the sand and he led her to his '72 Nova and she strode to the passenger side, fluttering her eyes coquettishly. Joey got in and turned the key, revved the engine and its shaking and burping and farting all over the place and she shot a loud roar out of her tailpipe and tore ass across the lot. Shelly grabbed the sidebar and the excitement lit up her thighs and they shuddered with the roar of the engine and she spread her legs apart, pushing them outward— but slowly, pressing her palms against the inner the thighs, slowly dragging them upward toward her throbbing centripetal force, and opened the window and.

THE HOT NIGHT SUMMER AIR.

When Shelly and Joey entered the diner, they chose the booth with the window facing Main Street and Shelly got the challah bread French toast, silver dollar pancakes, scrambled eggs with cheese and coffee with extra cream and sugar packets and Joey picked from her plate.

Why are ya nails painted black? she asked.

Ah, they're all fuckedup underneath, that's why.

Joey laughed and lit a Camel.Shelly slid a quarter in the juke box and told him her Aunt Mary used to sing her this song when she a was a kid, Blue Bayou.

I feel so bad I got a worried mind
I'm so lonesome all the time
Since I left my baby behind
On Blue Bayou

. . .

I'd be crying and all upset, missing my parents, and she'd be babysitting, trying to watch some TV show, annoyed as hell, probably, and she'd put on that record by Ronstadt and sing it to me—

I'm going back some day
Come what may
To Blue Bayou
Where the folks are fun
And the world is mine—

Three girls filed passed their booth and she recognized them from Buffalo, they recognized her, and the waitress led them to a round table in the center of the room and the Hispanic girl, Rosa, stared her down. She nudged her friends, Tessy and Marie. Shelly saw this and her heart fluttered up her throat, forcing out a cough, so she crossed over to the other side of the booth and slid next to him, draping her arm around his shoulders.

Pretend you're my boyfriend; she smiled, grabbing his hand and interlocking their fingers.

Joey examined her hand and the tiny freckles on the top of her hand and fingers and followed them all the way up her arm, on the sides of her neck, and delicate clavicle and how they thickened in clusters on her cheeks and the bridge of her nose. She confided in him that she never had a real boyfriend, and a blistering array of emotions overwhelmed her eyes and she squeezed the top of his leg then brushed her knuckles over his crotch. He squirmed and shifted his legs. She flattened her hand there and gave it a squeeze and watched his pupils constrict.

The laughter and giggling and the clanking of plates, and waitresses yelled orders and their serving bells rang, and the silverware rattled; songs from jukeboxes changed over, cash registers went *cha-chinge;* all the bustling noises seemed to assuage the sense of anxiety. She pushed her half eaten French toast to the side and took a gulp of coffee.

Why doya keep lookin over ya shoulder? Joey asked, turning his head to the giggling girls, who in turn gazed back at him, smiling, coyly batting their lids, and Rosa mouthed the words *handsome*, and Shelly saw this in the reflection of the window and bit down on her tongue until she tasted blood. Joey asked if she knew those girls and Shelly nodded her head, leering at the refection once again, noticing their simpering derision.

They see me in the reflection looking back at them, said Shelly. I know what they're saying. I can feel their thoughts and.

What a burnout.

Eighteen goin on fifty.

Look at'a dress.

Ugly cunt.

Picked that right off the rack at the Good Will.

Didn't she use'ta fuck Jordan for drugs or sumptin?

YA, YA—she fucked'm and he told everyone her cunt stunk like a swamp'a dead fish. Okay, okay, STOP. I'm ready to chuckup my omelette.

Fish Skins! HA-HA!

She was always a loser. I heard no one but Billy and Jordan went to'a sweet sixteen.

YA, YA—remember those invitations?

Oh-my-God how can I fuckin forget those. She mailed'm out to, like, everyone in the whole school, and they were all formal and shit, with her name in that awful gold script writing. How TACKY. Ya gotta be kiddin! Like, why the fuck ya inviting me? I'm actually offended.

YA, YA— and why doya have our addresses? Do we look like we have any drugs? Whatta loser.

Everyone laughed at those invites.

Fuckin freak.

And where'd she find this bum?

Probably at the Good Will.

Goddamn child molester. What is he? Thirty? Thirty-five?

I'm betting forty at least.

Let's get'm to look over at us. We'll flirt and call'm over right in front of'a.

How much ya wanta bet I can suck his cock by the end'a the night? How much? Huh?

I'm a lil dizzy.

We can leave.

I just hafta go ta the bathroom and I'll be okay.

Shelly squeezed her hands together, popped each knuckle on her right hand, then took a gulp of coffee and drag of Camel in effort alleviate the dizziness and divert her mind from the nausea. She was determined to ignore it.

I'll be okay. Lemme go get my bag and we'll get outta here.

Shelly passed the round table of girls and headed to the coat rack where her JanSport hung. Joey took another peek at the table of young ladies and watched them talk amongst themselves, eating; drinking, laughing, and Shelly returned, sat down, bag slung over one shoulder. He watched her take one drag of a cigarette after another, dumping one packet of sugar in her coffee after another, chewing her nail beds, ripping at her cuticles, biting her upper lip, glancing at the reflection in the window, then peeking over her shoulder and grimacing, soundlessly moving her mouth and.

Joey called the waitress over and asked for the check. Without looking at the bill, he brought the check up to the well-dressed Greek lady at the register and paid. Shelly remained seated, her back to the girls, and each time she felt her head turn, even the slightest, or glance in the reflection, she talked herself down, and took another drag, or another gulp of coffee, and redirected her thoughts and the worries and the what-if's would plague her mind indefinitely with terrible unrest and.

Joey watched her as he received change from the Greek lady and from that distance she radiated a unique beauty and gracefulness with her gentle movements. Although she's plagued with excessive worry and compulsive tics, there's a femininity and adroit usefulness of her fingers and the way they moved lithely over her neck, face, through her hair and back down the opposite side of her face, pulling the loose curly strands to her chin, then elevating her neck, closing her eyes, and flexing her jaw, as if posing for a photographer which only existed in her mind.

Joey folded the cash in his wallet, never taking his eyes off her, and walked back to the booth, threw down a $5 tip, grabbed her hand and walked out, passing the round table of girls, and pirouetting waitresses and busboys, and the drunks on the swivel stool at the cafe bar, and the crowd of teens stumbling in the EXIT, and the cook smashed the bell with his palm and screamed PICKUP, and the dishes and coffee mugs clanked and the jukeboxes ROARED.

As they approached the Nova, a voice yelled out and Joey turned, and the three girls from the round table stood just inches before him.

GIMME BACK MY BAG, FAGGAT, said Rosa.

Joey flipped his hands up, perplexed. Shelly came around the other end of the car, clutching the straps of her backpack.

Take my bag off your shoulder and give it back, ya little fuckin skank.

Whatta ya mean? This is my bag.

NO, that's *my* bag, said Rosa, as she approached them. Shelly took a step back.

Then show me what's in the bag then, said Rosa, snapping her head to one side.

I'm ain't showin you shit.

Joey stepped between them.

She had that bag when she came in, he said.

Rosa yelled at Shelly and called her a piece of shit junky.

FUCK OFF!

Marie spat in Joey's face, and Rosa rapped him on the cheek, digging, then dragging her gold rings into his cheekbone, and Joey dragged them to the ground, and Rosa dug her teeth into his shoulder, and Shelly came around the car and kicked Marie, upturning her face, and Shelly stomped and kicked her some more, and Tessy, screamed and screamed and the waitstaff ran out, and onlookers gathered in the windows, peeking between the vertical blinds, and the waiter yanked Rosa off Joey while grabbing her tits and smiling at the other waiters, who winked, and the Greek lady called the cops, and Rosa spat at Joey again, and Joey took both hands and cupped them over Rosa's mouth, and Tessy jumped on his back and Rosa kicked him between the legs, and Shelly grabbed a giant clump of Marie's hair, while her free hand formed a fist and smashed the back of Marie's skull over and over, and when her knuckles began cracking, she used the heel of her hand and focused on the side of Marie's face, bashing her ear until the warm wetness of Marie's blood splashed over her palm and dribbled down her wrist and Marie grabbed a hold of Shelly's legs pulled them in and Shelly lost her balance but did not fall and.

COPS.

TWO POLICE CARS. FOUR COPS

Tore Shelly off Marie, tore Rosa and Tessy off Joey, and Joey swung blindly, and the cop knocked him on his ass with one swing of the baton, cuffed him, hands behind his back, and pulled Joey to his knees and left him there while they broke apart Shelly and Marie. Marie put up no struggle and cried, hands in the air, promising not to swing or hurt anyone and.

THEY STOLE MY FUCKIN BAG I SWEAR TA GOD!

I DID NOT! THAT'S MY BAG!

One cop checked everyone's ID and Shelly would not break eye contact from Marie, who then suddenly doubled over and puked in the bushes. The cop picked up the JanSport bag from ground and held it up, and Rosa yelled to check inside

THERE'S THREE BEEPERS, SOME MAKEUP AND A PACK OF NEWPORTS.

The cop unzipped the bag, dug through the bag, and the onlookers waited, and Joey, still cuffed, on knees, waited (the pebbles dug out his knee caps and he shifted his weight to the back of his heels) and the cop looked up from the bag, eyes blanked over, and then looked to Shelly and Rosa, and slid out a blue leather address book, and said there was nothing in the bag that fit her description. The welts swelled on Marie's face and blood trickled from her ear, and Rosa stayed staring at Shelly, and Tessy stayed staring at the ground. Joey asked if they could remove the cuffs, and the cop stood him up and unlocked the cuffs while asking how many years he served in the Marines, and Joey rubbed his wrists, smoothing the skin over, increasing circulation, and said 4 years, and the cop handed him back his wallet and said he was in the Corp too.

Whatta ya do now? asked the cop.

I'm a dock builder.

Oh, Union 1556?

That's the one.

You know Bob Healey?

That's my boss.

That's my cousin.

Joey nodded his head and continued to rub his wrists.

The cop handed him back his Military ID and license, then directed his attention to Shelly, who sat on the curb, head between knees. He placed a latex glove on each hand.

Hi, Shelly I'm just gonna check ya out. I wanta make sure you're okay. Can ya lift your head of me?

Shelly lifted her head. The cop shined his light on her and observed raised welts that streaked the sides of her face and chest.

I'm okay. I just wanta go home, that's all, said Shelly, trying to control her anger and the nausea.

The officer said okay, then turned to Joey and asked him if he was aware she was a minor, and he told him he had no idea, that he just met her.

Be careful, the cop said in a low voice.

I'm takin'a home and that's that.

The cop said okay and headed back to the other group where the officers continued to keep the girls calm. Rosa held an ice pack over her ear, complaining the white bitch ripped her earring out, and she'll get hers. The cop told her to keep quite or else.

THE NOVA EXITED THE PARKING LOT

Shelly sat there. Bolt upright. Not moving. The frayed strands of yellow curls covering her face, the sweat burning the scratches along her cheeks and chest, and the voices and transmissions, and cop engines roared to life. Her head swelled and throbbed, and the gnawing pit in the center of her chest would not stop drumming, and she raked the sides of her legs with her nails, her eyes were lost in the Highway.

Any long, bumpy rides were sure to make her stomach sick and uneasy and she was surprised she didn't throw up, and she was surprised she wasn't shaking, but calming. Her leg and arm muscles calming, the labored breathing and heart returning to sinus rhythm, and her facial muscles calming and lids closing, and when they got to the beach, the water was calming, soothing them both and pulling away the negative energy and the moon upon the water glittering and reflecting...

WHITELIGHT

All the hate and all the hurt had partially left her body. For the moment. Before she opened the door to get out, she said it's okay if he never wanted to see her again because of all the trouble she caused him for the night. And she understood if he didn't, but it hurt her to think this, and even more to say it, because the reality of the moment had really set in, and she knew he wouldn't want to deal with a tragedy case like her on the regular. She went on and said she totally understood—

Joey didn't bother to listen to the rest. He looked to her legs and the open wounds and skin tags and one streak of dribbling blood running down her shin. He saw the pain from the aftermath of the night stinging her guts and those soft baby girl eyes, and he just blurted it out:

I'm havin a few people over this weekend, if ya wanta stop by. Nothin big, just a few close friends.

She smiled and squirmed and he told her lived at the Pinewood Apartments down in the village. She knew exactly where it was. Apartment #9.

She gave him a quick peck on the cheek and got out. The Nova ROARED to life.

EARLY MORNING— CLINIC.

Shelly lined up for the orange-colored concoction of methadone hydrochloride and Tang. In a ritual of relief, she gulped "the medication" in child-sized plastic cups. She winced and walked out. She skipped her appointment with Maryann and went to the mall. She sat on the edge of the indoor water fountain, lit a cigarette and smiled. Today, she was finally happy.

Billy sauntered by, holding a shopping bag, oblivious to everything. She yelled out his name, but he kept going. She knew he heard her. She saw that sideway glance as he cut through a pair of Mom's with strollers.

BILLY!

BILLY!

BILLY!

Vanished in the faceless crowd of the many. The chest throbbed for him and she didn't quite know why. A connection reeling backward to childhood? A rejection that hurt worse than any punch or insult. Her heart, voidlike and dull. The happiness drained through her and did not return.

She spent the rest of the afternoon walking numbly through the mall and visited Tape World. Found Souvlaki and The Real Ramona in the used bin. Tapes she's been after for a while. Slide them up her sleeve and walked right out the fucking door.

LATER THAT NIGHT…

. . .

Movie time with Mother. Some weirdo foreign movie with a title she'll never remember. She couldn't follow the storyline because of all those distracting subtitles. Her eyes bounced from the faces of the movie actors, to the words, the picture of the blessed Mother on the end table. The Rosary beads around the picture. Then back to the movie. More words to a scene she could care less about. But Mother was hooked. Eyes aligned. Shelly nodded and finally slept.

The end credits rolled until the tape clicked, and auto-rewind clicked, and the mechanical high speed WOOOOOOOOOSSSSSH-HHHHHHHHHHHHHHHHHHHHHHHHHHHED.

Shelly awoke.

10PM.

Mother was snoring next to her, sitting up. She almost looked awake. Her lids fluttering, half opened. The urge to see Joey again was slightly less than the urge she felt for the junk, but still strong enough to take Mother's car after she'd fallen asleep. She tiptoed to the door and looked once more at Mother on the couch. She dressed, took money, and the keys from Mother's purse and left. When she stood on the porch the moon looked familiar as it did the night she met him at the swingset. And nothing else mattered.

Take the car, said Mother from the screen door.

Shelly froze. Her legs stiffened.

All ya hafta do is ask, baby. I know ya need ta see ya friends.

Shelly turned to Mother, not fully taking in the moment. Not fully believing her.

I can't hold on ta ya forever.

A sad smile lifted Shelly's face.

If ya ever need ta talk, I'm here for ya, okay?

Shelly nodded. Mother's eyes, wet and swollen. She waved and disappeared into the darkness of the house. The door shut.

. . .

Shelly pulled up to Joey's apartment and rang the bell. Voices hushed and mellowed as the footsteps came to the door. Deadbolt unlocked. Smoke and light flooded her face.

HEYA SHELL, said Joey surprised.

WHATS UP? S'OKAY I'M HERE?

YEAH, YEAH COME ON IN. JUST A COUPLA PEOPLE OVA.

Shelly entered a small gathering. An older lady on a couch, grinding her jaw, lounging next to a biker in a leather vest with long braided hair, and a younger blonde girl sitting Indian style in the center of the room, hypnotized by the TV screen, unaware of everything.

THAT'S ADIE ON THE COUCH AND STEVE NEXT TA HER. AND THIS IS MARCY. EVERYONE THIS IS SHELLY.

No one said a word… then…

How old'a ya doll? asked Adie.

Shelly looked to Joey and winked, said "Eighteen."

Christ. She's a fuckin child, snorted Adie.

Steve glared.

Marcy said nothing.

Yeah well, I'm an old soul.

I've heard that one before, laughed Steve.

Adie elbowed him in the gut.

Hang out. Sit down, said Joey.

Adie reached into her purse and pulled out a glass bowl and unfolded a baggie with rocks. She put one in the bowl and heated it up and.

Joey diverted Shelly by talking and giving her the tour of his studio and there ain't much to see aside from the Komodo dragon terrarium and one overstuffed bookshelf. The bowl passed to Marcy and she drew in a big inhale and her eyes inflated then sauntered over and gave it to Steve and he inhaled and choked and his eyes fluttered and gave it back to Adie and.

Shelly received a cigarette from Joey and lit it and leaned back in the chair, closed her eyes, felt the tension increase in her legs and allowed her body to shake, and asked what's that on the coffee table. A mirror with lines of powder and the particles in the air gave Shelly a sudden rush and a sore throat and she gulped a cup of water Joey gave her and he told her the powder was coke and asked if she wanted some. Adie shook her head and said it ain't for kids and Shelly bragged she's in a treatment program for dope and that impressed them and she pressed her nose flat saying the bone rotted from sniffing all the H for years and they rolled eyes and made gestures with their hands and jabbered and giggled as she snorted a line and opened her eyes tragically, her arms shaking, hanging limply, whispering to Joey and brushing off questions, bobbing her head slowly, taking a drag. Joey put on some coffee and her hands and feet tingled, her heart pounded, and she extinguished a cigarette and lit another as he put on a record and Shelly didn't know who it was and they all laughed, spinning round and round and the music pumped and Adie asked why she hadn't heard of The Doors. Shelly shrugged and said because they probably sucked and Steve laughed harder saying he saw these guys live in '69 and they ain't no joke and that dude was off his fuckin rocker man, far out there, further out there then you'll ever be little girlie. He whipped out his cock on stage and told everyone ta suck it! and Shelly's eyes bugged and Joey brought over a cup of coffee for Adie and Shelly and she gulped it and did another line. Adie, Steve and Joey sung along with NOT TO TOUCH THE EARTH and Shelly squealed and said she liked the sound of that guy's voice!

NOW YA TALKIN! said Steve.

And Shelly did another line and plopped next to Marcy who finally came alive and they talked and shared stories and Marcy was a dancer at club Eden and Shelly should come down some day, because—

You are gorgeous!

Joey rubbed the powder over his gums and laughed and Shelly grabbed another cup of coffee and told her she looked just like a little fairy and.

We're all dead fairies in the end… that's all we are; dead

fairies, she said and no one laughed or made a joke but changed the subject. Shelly spotted a book on an ottoman with an interesting cover. She picked it up, opened it, flipped through a few pages and just decided to read—

"You have only wasted your life!"

The first words jumped out and rang through the room, above the talking of others, above the song changing to the next song, and she read louder

(Ah, that was the knife!)

When I rushed through the garden gate

It was all too late.

And Adie and Steve moved their eyes toward her

Could we live it over again

Were it worth the pain,

Could the passionate past that is fled

Call back its dead!

They were all watching her now, especially Marcy. They were finally all looking at her, like she was a STAR.

Well, if my heart must break,

Dear love, for your sake,

It will break in music, I know,

Poet's hearts break so.

Joey, a stone statue, lost in the theatrics of the moment, could not unglue his eyes from this dramatic presence, and her chest swelled and the poem came forth with beauty and grace, her voice soft and melodious.

But strange that I was not told

That the brain can hold

In a tiny ivory cell

God's heaven and hell.

She sank down in the couch, the book falling to her lap, the words still ringing in her ears like the waves down at the beach, repeating, God's heaven and hell. The candles flickered and soon went out. Shelly clutched her chest, heart racing and the pain, that dull, horrible, nauseous pain, ate away at her chest, and the flapping and the furious flapping wings roared through the room, and she descended to darkness without control, and the voices panicked and increased in decibels before they finally fell as soft as snow, and the silence. The SILENCE. And the fear lifted and no longer tore away at her. Shelly's legs loosened and arms dropped and she faintly smelled the grass and felt its wet dew under her and.

SHE'S OKAY SHE'S OKAY, said Joey, hugging/rocking her.

His long hair fell upon her face, and for a moment, her eyes opened only to close once more and.

Decedent at friend's house when she "passed out". Friend dragged Decedent outside onto lawn and performed CPR. When Decedent was unresponsive, friend called 911 from payphone then left due to outstanding warrants. Paramedics arrived on scene, advanced cardiac life support was initiated, transported to emergency room where she was pronounced dead. History of heroin abuse.

WELCOME TO EDEN

SEGUE #2

CHAPTER 4

THE CRONIES CHORUS

MARCY

Rubbed her ass all over Mackey's crotch. He grabbed the sides of the couch and held on. She spun around, opened his legs, and jammed a knee between them. Rubbed the knee up and down the long, hard outline of his shaft, while looking in his eyes. His hands released the cushions and one slid up her ribs, going for her tits. She grabbed his hand.

NOPE.

She straddled his legs, moving her cunt up and down over his cock. The wetness bleeding through the pink G-string.

Oh, come onnnnnnnn… not nothin? he asked, and squeezed her ass.

Hands ta yaself, said Marcy, and pointed to the sign which read: HANDS OFF THE DANCERS.

Only I do the touchin, handsome, she said, caressing his face with her other hand.

Ya gonna make me fuckin cum, he muttered.

Good.

Faster, he groaned, running out of breath.

She did.

He looked her in the face and said, you're like everythin I

want in a lady… yknow that? Your fuckin eyes, tits, those fuckin strong-ass legs—

She put her knee back to his cock. Her thigh muscle contracting, flexing, as she continued to massage the shaft, in circular gyrations.

Everything… fuckin goddess… ya know that?

Marcy smiled and licked his chin—

NOT TOO CLOSE, said Steve from the doorway.

Tell that fuckin guy ta turn around or sumptin, he's killin it fa me.

I can't… and if I were you, I wouldn't be a tough guy in here.

Her knee came up a bit so the thigh blocked Steve's view… and her left hand grabbed the shaft and slid up and down…his arms stiffened… he grabbed her ankle, the gold anklet fit tight and perfect. He studied the arches of her feet. Bits of saliva dripped off his tongue and over his lips. One more sharp intake of breath…and she finished him off. His arms fell loose. She stayed over him, watching his expression change, loving the power she exuded over him.

I'm havin some people over tonight at my aunt's cabin out east, he said. You should come by. No, I *need* ya ta come by.

She smiled. Can't. Workin till 4am.

Come onnnnnnnn… Just gonna be a few people. Ya party?

Marcy stood up and asked, Meaning what?

I got E, K, dust, dope, whatever. Whatta ya into?

Yeah? You sell?

He nodded, adjusting his fly and belt.

What about rock?

Got that, too.

What if I wanted ta bring a couple friends? Whudya have enough?

Mackey looked around and bent over his knapsack. He unzipped it and moved his hand inside, stirring up Ziploc bags of E pills, dope, and packets of dust.

What would possess ya ta bring all that in here?

Cause I don't give a fuck.

She lit up a cigarette and blew smoke in his face and glowed, You're a bold little boy.I ain't no boy, he whispered, throwing the knapsack over his shoulder. He took a wad of cash and peeled off a 50. Handed to her. Smiled.

She smiled back and told him to leave her the address to his aunt's.

And he did.

PART THREE
LIQUID SHADE

He who binds to himself a joy
Does the winged life destroy;
But he who kisses the joy as it flies
Lives in eternity's sun rise.

—William Blakc, Etcrnity

CHAPTER 5
CLUB KIDS

LIQUID SHADE

—A dingy nightclub down the bowels of Long Island. A real filth hole that had all the good stuff and music you'd never hear or see anywhere else in the suburbs, especially in '93. It's a place where you'd smell the crack-chlorine aroma the second you stepped inside. You knew… Hell was there, and real, and when you'd get the E inside it'd turn to sweet heaven, melting, sweaty, dripping, hot, cold, jaw grinding, shirt pulling, face touching, stranger fucking, gender bending, androgynous humans transcending all forms of normality and what you thought at one time made up the safe real world was full of enough shit to fill the oceans.

THE MUSIC

Hard, heavy music of mechanical beats. The songstress of the streets. The melody of the dead, palliate the dead with its song, the bitterness of scumfucks and whores, the unearthing of the melody that creates the storm which rocks the race.

Space glissandos echoing and liquid synth chords dripping around the tribal drums.

Can't you see I wanna be with youuuuuu, sang the black woman's voice from the speakers.

wanna be
wanna be
wanna be with youuuuuuuuuuuuu
Can't you see I wanna be with youuuuu
wanna be
wanna be be be be be

The drum rolls and snapping snares battling with the female voice wrapped them up in the otherworldly arms of sound that'll hug you and be good to you as the shit hits your system and your skin turns to ice.

They were good there… too good… they never wanted to leave. How could you want to leave when the tingling ecstasy floods your groin, bursts up from the bowels, and tickles every inch of skin with the feather of eternal pleasure? So it seems. You come back down. You crash. You crash hard. And everything is shit again. But at you least you had that taste of heaven.

OUTSIDE ON THE DECK

Victor got the first bump of meth. A lightning jolt shot up to his brain and almost burned the poor bastard's eyes out of his head. Heather reached over and pinched his side and licked his neck.

THE BACK ROOM

Jonathan sat transfixed by an exotic Hispanic woman with long curly hair, a silver shiny dress, gliding over his dick, pulling on his hair, biting his earlobe. His hands all over her thighs and ass, grabbing and squeezing, a finger crawling closer to the center, moving the underwear over, feeling the warmth of her cunt—

Seth sat beside him, pinned to the same couch, tripping his face off. His hand reaching for the Hispanic woman, moving up her dress. Feeling around there. The smooth, roundness of her ass—

Chris and Mackey, dusted beyond worlds, pointed and sneered at these two fools, but all they had was each other.

SYMPHONY AND TROY

Locked in a bathroom stall, on a toilet set, her finger digging up his ass as she sucked him off, gagging herself, going as deep as she could (in both orifices). Troy grabbed her short, boy-cut raven hair and yanked her up, clapped both hands on each side of her face and got inside her mouth with his tongue.

CHRIS AND MACKEY

Wandered outside. The old broken down school bus turned lounge, sprouted kids like dandelion weeds across an open field. Smoke plumes rose from the windows. Rayanne glided over on her skateboard, popped off, and hugged Chris, nearly knocking the cane out of his hand. She sniffed the side of face and giggled coquettishly, grazing the tiny hairs on the back of his neck with her hand. Chris kissed her forehead. Mackey wandered off, watching them black clouds swirl around the moon.

JONATHAN

Flexed his pelvis deeper in the Spanish girl's ass as it moved in circles. She whipped round and round and faced him, dragging her face along his cheek, the sweat off her skin dribbling like tears. Jonathan licked them off and tasted the sweetness. He dug both hands down the back of her skirt, and scratched upward. She moaned in his ear, the treble of her voice tickling his skin, vibrating up and down his neck. The acid hit his brain at that moment and he saw stars. A rush of adrenalin burned along the top his chest and shoulders. He thought his bones would burst through his body. She pushed him back and the claustrophobia mounted as the blood pumped through his heart; he wanted it to pound hard - HARD. She squealed and opened her eyes and the strobes flashed and fluttered blue, green, red, STOPPED, then swirled and flashed again. The other dancers waved arms and stuttered movements between the lights. Strings and synths pushed waves of motion though the sweaty bodies, giving them a surge of power on the smoky floor.

Seth rubbed a hand over his crotch and unzipped his jeans, watching Jonathan get dry-fucked by the Latina. He watched the slow circular movements of her ass, the way her thighs spread over his lap, as he straightened slightly against the couch.

She put her mouth against Jonathan's ear and said

WAS THERE EVERY A BETTER FEELIN THAN THIS?

He said no, and put his mouth over hers and grabbed a handful of her hair, twisting it between his fingers.

TROY AND SYMPHONY

Sat in the bathroom against the wall, watching the others come and go, and their grinding jaws and shivering lips, Troy leaned his head against hers and told her how much he loved her and she jammed her tongue in his ear, and he clenched his teeth, grinding his molars and shook from ribs, exhaling, and inhaling, feeling the euphoric surge. He wanted to love Symphony for the rest of her life and have many babies and he told her this, and she believed him.

You won't hafta work no more. I'll take care'a ya. I'll get two jobs if I hafta. You just stay home and I'll come home to you every day and give ya nuttin but love, and give our family nuttin but love, and we'll lay in bed at night, just holding, rubbing, touching, fucking...

And she nodded and he jabbered away, rubbing the top of her hands, then palms, ticking there, playfully, grabbing her leg and placing it over his.

You don't know how much I love ya, Symphony. I can't find

out how ta tell ya. I can't find out the words and make em tell ya exactly what I'm feelin right now.

And she agreed saying, I know, I know, I know— her teeth grinding like creaking wood.

Ya want my babies? she asked.

I want all your babies. I wanta deliver them then crawl back up inside your cunt and live there and be a part'a ya, and ya, ya, ya, I want all your babies ALL OF EM... BE WITH ME? BE WITH ME? SAY IT!

Be with you, said Symphony nodding and nodding

Stay with me?

Stay with you FOR-EVER.

Ever and ever?

Ever and EVER AND EVER AND EVER EVER FOREVER-RRRRRRRRRRRRRRRR!

Don't ever leave me, said Troy in between kisses, and his eyes rolled and lids fluttered.

Symphony wrapped her arms around him, shaking and biting his bottom lip and rubbing his shoulders, feeling the muscles contract and loosen.

IN THE LIZARD ROOM...

Abstract darkness, lit only by the fluorescent lights of the cages of Komodo dragons and iguanas. Chris and Mackey scanned the floor with mini-flashlights, giggling, shoving, and tripping one another up. Chris zeroed in on a plastic bag in the corner and swiped it up, giggling. Mackey kicked him in the tailbone as he got up and sent him back down again, right on his ass.

FAGGAT!

Mackey kicked him again, leaving a sneaker imprint on his chest.

FAGGAT FAGGAT FAGGAT! said Chris, having a hard time catching his breath. Mackey dropped on a couch and opened his knapsack, peeked inside, wanted to have another look at all the E pills and Acid in little baggies, wrapped in one larger Ziploc baggie. Chris sat next to him.

Whatta ya think it is? asked Mackey.

Dunno, he shrugged.

Chris squeezed the sides of the little baggie open, dipped in his index finger, and tasted. His face crinkled.

I think it's K?

Then Mackey tapped a bump on his knuckle and snorted it.

Yup. It's K. Whooaaaaaaaaaaaaaaaaaaaaaaa.

Mackey grabbed the bag and copied Tarik.

A FEW MINUTES LATER...

Both staring at the ceiling, holding their backpacks against their chest, mouths hung open like zombies. Kids passing, sitting, talking, laughing, smoking, drinking, and Chris and Mackey remained staring into the vacuous abyss of a K-Hole, thinking of nothing, cut off from thought and feeling anything.

Mackey twitched his lips and raised a finger up to point at something traveling by that only he could see, and this traveling something he followed until it landed just above the head of a girl who took the seat next to him. His finger nearly touched the tip of her nose. The girl went cross-eyed. Mackey's head drooped to his chest, out cold. Chris still stared at nothing, half-lidded and blanked over.

ON THE DANCE FLOOR...

Heather watched Victor caught in a dance battle between two break-dancers, one spinning wildly on the floor and one, mechanically and robotically shuffling his feet and slicing hand movements like Kung-Fu in Victor's face. A black girl, lithe like a ballerina, spun between them all and ducked her head behind her arms like a boxer covering up from punches, lunging her face out, then back behind her arms, then out, then in, and reached back to her knapsack and pulled out a small bottle of baby powder and shook it up. Plumes of powder dusted the air, caught in the strobe and dry ice fog, landing on the floor, easing the dancer's feet in syncopation with the beats, rattling the chest, skull, and every fiber in the body, all of it, buzzing and humming. Victor backed out of the circle because he couldn't keep up with these guys and girls. This was their life— dancing, partying, battling— they were the real G's of the club and what they did, how they expressed themselves through movement, it was law.

BUT JONATHAN AND SETH

Were winding down, man, and that Latina wouldn't let up. She was flipping out on some bender and just wouldn't come down. Just wouldn't. Seth came all over his hands and pants and zipped it up and dried his hands along the sides of his jeans on the edges of the couch. That Latin girl pulled Jonathan's hair straight up like Don King, so he patted it back in place and he was still bugging with those googly eyes and nervous face. Mackey and Chris walked by with their flashlights, still in a zone, not totally out of it. The effects wore off some, but they were walking by and they saw these two clowns—still pinned to the cushions like a couple of decorations, watching this wild ass Latina shake her shit— and just ROARED with laughter. Especially Mackey, shining his flashlight all over Jonathan's face, keeping it in his eyes, and he didn't know whether he was coming or going, and the light just added to his lunacy and disorientation. He covered his eyes, swatting the light away, twitching, not knowing why this light kept blinding him. Then Chris got his light on Seth and it freaked him the fuck out man, because that kid just looked dead. Expressionless, eyes closed, slumped over like a weed, hand curled like it was holding something that just got away. But he moved. Chris held the light there long enough to watch him come alive, notice them, and wrap his arms around himself like a straitjacket and hug himself - really

HUGGED HIMSELF TIGHTLY - and Chris and Mackey sung End of the Road:

Although we've come
To the end of the road
Still I CAN'T LET GO
It's unnatural
You belong to me
I belong to youuuuuuuuuuuu

Chris snaked his arm around Seth and Mackey yanked the top of Jonathan's head, pulling his hair way high and they roared with laughter—

TROY AND SYMPHONY

Made their way out of the bathroom, arms around one another, embraced as if they were fused together at the seams of their shoulders and thighs, walking side by side. Troy's goatee tickling her neck, sucking in his bottom lip, biting down on his labret stud, pushing it deeper into his chin. The strobes fucking them up, fucking up their eyesight and Troy stumbled back and his eyes did a flutter, almost rolled to the back of his skull, and Symphony felt his body tug away and she looked over at him

Hey, hey, hey! Troy! Troy! she slurred, slapping his face. Stay with me… stay with me, man.

She bit his cheek playfully. Troy jerked around, startled by the sudden bite and he managed to pull up a smile.

VICTOR WATCHED HEATHER

On the dance floor, her turn now, her turn to unleash the bottled up vitality of youth mixed with narcotics and blood, sweat, and tears and throw her body around like it was some flimsy piece of rubber. Contorting into movement that appeared unnatural and not humanly possible, but the flickering strobe and smoke made her into an ethereal dance goddess too pure for this world and he believed it, watching the majestic site, stoned off his ass on meth—

TROY GRABBED SYMPHONYS HAND

My heart, my heart, can ya feel my heart? Is it still there?

She placed her ear to his chest and said yes it's still there and it's beating REALLY fucking hard—

Well how come I can't feel it if it's beating so fucking hard!

JONATHAN GRABBED SETH

And said, All my world WHY! Deeper inside I wonder in this world of fuckin anger— WHY! I ask of that question—

And Seth turned to Chris and pulled out a pen from his knapsack and said, I'm gonna stab this muthafucka in the neck. Get em away!

Chris laughed and said, DO IT!

Jonathan reached out for the Latina— still twisting and shaking her ass like a madwoman possessed by some holy ghost at a gospel church, throwing hallelujahs and amens from the chest heavenward, heavenward— and got her down so they were face to sweaty face. Her sweat breaking off, splashing onto his eyes, burning them— but he didn't give no shit— and he became fascinated by the size of her breasts, when she turned they seemed to follow a few seconds later, the hard dark nipples poking out through the dress and he said to her

Fuckin QUEEN! FUCK MY SOUL YOU FUCKIN QUEEN— IT'S REAL. I'M CRAZY BUT REAL. FOLLOW THE TRAIL DOWN TO THE SPARROW TAIL. I RUN IN CIRCLES, I FIND IT. Strobe light of hell, give me power to love this beautiful fuckin QUEEN of the AMAZON. Oh God, hear me. I love you. I feel ashamed but quite cool. I'm insensitive, but a FOOL!

DON'T YOU EVER SAY THAT! said the Latina through tight lips. DON'T YOU EVER EVER SAY THAT! YOU ARE BEAUTIFUL!

And she caressed his face with her hand, the long, thin fingers and long thin blood-red nails tracing his cheek and rolling her tongue over his ear, biting the lobe, bits of saliva dripping, then penetrating his ear canal—

I am a fool, he whispered. The tongue on my ear is good. I sweat the snake's drool. So smooth, so… help me god… fuck me god… help me… you're my god… you're my god… YOU'RE MY CULT—

She unlatched his belt and shoved her hand down his pants.

MEANWHILE…

TROY AND SYMPHONY

Sat on a big speaker and Troy's throat contracted, coughing up saliva and he told her he needed water, NOW!

Symphony split and reached the bar and slammed down $2 and said lemme have a bottle, NOW! And she got her bottle and ran back to Troy but Troy had already split and now she had to find him through the throngs of kids and more kids. Some holding skateboards ready to hop on the halfpipe outside, some enveloped to one another like her and Troy once were, some cracked out on crazy benders, feeling each other up, pulling hair, clasped hands, dancing, kissing, touching, loving madly and wildly and the music won't stop and none of this will stop for anyone. It's a sad, sick, violent march, a parasitic promenade of pesky insects marching along in sweet holy hell. She reached through the crowds and everywhere she turned she thought she saw him, that oversized fleece and long, sweeping jeans frayed at the bottoms, sweeping the floor.

FUCK! WHERE ARE YOU! she screamed, eyes afloat with tears.

· · ·

HEATHER FINALLY RESTED

In a quiet, cozy corner writing in a small spiral notepad, while Victor took his turn dancing his ass off no more than a few feet from her—

Dear Victor,4/9/93

Hey my love, what's going down? Nothing interesting for me right now, just watching ya and falling even deeper for ya—if that's even possible. Ya know what? <u>I love you a lot</u>. Do me a favor, let's forget about what happened last night because I understand that you didn't realize what you were doing, so we are going to forget all about it.

Victor, I love you so much & I'm never going to leave you. Never ever. And pretty soon we will be living together and soon after that we will get married. I can't wait to sleep w/you and wake up w/you and lay w/you all the time.

<u>I LOVE YOU ALWAYS</u>,

Heather.

CHRIS AND MACKEY

Had to make a decision. Both these guys locked themselves in a bathroom stall. Mackey holding the big Ziplock bag filled with pills.

How much ya got so far? asked Chris, leaning on his cane.

Coupla hundred. You?

Same.

Let's just cut out. Ain't nobody buyin, besides, that dancer might be stoppin by.

Word? You think so?

I dunno, maybe. I don't wanta miss out if she does, though. Troy knows how ta get ta my aunt's cabin out east. He's been there with me a bunch'a times.

Chris nodded, organizing the crumpled 5's, 10's, and 20's.

. . .

OUTSIDE…

Troy held onto the back of his car and puked his guts out. Symphony rubbed his back, still holding the water bottle. Troy finished up and sank down, shaking. She handed him the bottle, he brought it to his lips, took a gulp, swished it around and spat it out.

I haven't puked since I was fourteen, he said, shivering.

Too much, too much, it's just too much, said Symphony, rubbing the back of his neck.

I feel a little better, though. What time is it?

She looked down at her digital watch, A lil before 2.

A Nova rolled by, its engine grunting like a pig. She studied the car while acting like she wasn't.

INSIDE…

Jonathan finished his fate with the Latina by receiving her phone number on a tiny piece of white paper. She held his face in her hands and kissed his forehead before leaving.

Probably fake number, whispered Seth. Jonathan nodded, still mesmerized by her presence as she walked away, watching her hips, thighs, ass, remembering the softness and how she felt against him.

The two walked out onto the dance floor. Seth wandered ahead of him, blending with the many bodies, the darkness, the strobe, the flickering madness, and Jonathan got to the center of the dance floor and watched, nodded, and moved around a bit, but he didn't dance. The acid, still in his eyes and brain, the inflating pupils and elevated sense of euphoria. Chunks of time missing. Sped up, and then slowed down. He moved his feet around a bit, shuffling to the rhythms. The music tugged at his chest. Not wanting it end, yet knowing it had to at some point. A girl appeared before him, her face cut up in the strobe, her smile wide and filled with metal. She got close to his face and pressed her lips to his ear

Hey, doya have a girlfriend?

He shook his head.

See that girl over there? she asked, pointing over his shoulder. Jonathan looked in that direction and saw three girls standing near the bathrooms. The fluorescent light behind them.

Which one? asked Jonathan, pressing his lips to her ear.

The middle. The one in the middle. She wants ta know ya. Here, come with me, she said and grabbed his hand. They weaved among the kids and Jonathan seemed a bit off balance, swaying this way and that way, just sort of rolling along like a cloud in the sky.

The girl joined them by the hand and said

This is Elizabeth. Here, take her hand dummy. Jonathan did and leaned in and introduced himself, slurring his name. Never had he seen such crystal clear blue eyes and powdery white skin. He brushed her bangs off her brow.

I like your hair, he said.

She giggled, and told him it's mousey and she hates the color. He told her she looks like a STAR. Her teeth cracked open a smile, parting two cherry red lips.

VICTOR AND HEATHER

Sat against the wall, slumped into each other's lap. Victor caressing her head, kissing her hair. Chris came over and said

We're cuttin out.

Nah, man, not now… come back later.

Can you guys catch a ride with Symphony and Troy, then?

I haven't see'm all night. Whassup? asked Victor.

Look, we just gotta head out now, man.

Victor clucked his tongue and rolled his head, Fuck is up with this shit? I don't know where they're at?! I ain't leavin.

Then you on your own.

Well, that's really shitty, said Heather. Thanks a lot!

I just said we need ta bounce now and ya man ain't ready. I'm sayin if ya wanta come out east with us, we leavin now. Ya don't wanta come, catch a ride wit someone else.

Forget it, forget it, we'll come; we'll come, said Victor and he peeled himself off the floor and rose to his feet.

SYMPHONY AND TROY

Seats reclined. Hands held. Troy curled in fetal position. Symphony stared at him, worried. His breathing slow and shallow. His hands moist and cold.

That's it, I'm drivin us home. Ya can stay at my place.

Troy shifted and forced a smile.

Take me ta the beach, he said. I just wanta chill for a while.

Symphony told him fine and turned the key in the ignition and the engine ROARED to life.

JONATHAN AND ELIZABETH

Sat on a little deck, next to the magic bus. Elizabeth downed a bottle of a water. Her tiny hands trembled and so did her jaw.

Where'd ya go ta school? she asked him.

Buffalo. You? he asked in a soft, quite voice.

Inwood. I live out in C.I. with my mom and sisters now.

Jonathan nodded, smiled. He brushed her bangs out of her eyes again.

I wanta see'm, he said. They're soooooooooooo purdy.

You are, said Elizabeth.

Nope.

She leaned over, hand on his knee, staring at his pupils, watching them constrict, then dilate.

Well, I think you are, she finally said.

Jonathan rested his chin on his knees, looking at his Airwalks.

They're shredded from skating. Can almost see my toes.

Elizabeth giggled and said, They looked like they were once nice. She leaned closer.

What are ya on?

Just some acid, but it wore off. I took it way earlier. Whatta bout you?

Just some E. I only took half. I still have the other half if ya want it.

Jonathan looked back to his sneakers. He stretched out his legs and pointed his toes, and said, Yeah, okay.

Elizabeth smiled and reached into her knapsack...

IN THE VAN

Mackey gunned it down Sunrise Highway. The trees soared by. Chris passed out in the passenger's seat, and Heather lay across Victor's lap. The blackness of the sky lifting to a light purple on the horizon. A heavy weight seemed to be pressing on his lids and he felt his body become weightless, no arms, no legs— a floating eye watching himself drive, moving around the van to each area, then out on the highway, in front of the van, shifting upward, suspended in weightless space. The lightness of motion, of being suspended, filled his groin through the passage of endless time. The exits soared passed him. He reached down from space and the darkness separated and lightened, and both legs tingled and burned and he forced his eyes open, then squeezed them shut, trying to alleviate the dryness and he had become aware that his legs had fallen asleep. He tried to shake them awake. He blinked incessantly, and the highway lights filled his line of vision, breaking apart in tiny dots and pulsations.

AT THE BEACH

Blue sky coming through the darkness, but slowly, softly. Symphony looked up through the sunroof, her fingers tracing the palm of Troy's left hand. His eyes opened slightly, although still dark, the brightness of her eyes radiated. He lifted her hand to his mouth and kissed the knuckles, while smelling her skin.

. . .

JONATHAN

Swayed on the deck, face blazing with sweat, twisting a water bottle between his hands. Elizabeth bit his ear and licked up his neck and dug her nails into his thigh. His groin pulsed and blood flowed. The softness of her cheek against his, the sweat dripping from her brow down her cheek onto his lips. The grinding jaws, clenched fists, and he took her lip into his mouth. At that moment, Jonathan's stomach tightened and his mouth filled with saliva. He pulled back and began to swallow, forcing the lump back down his throat. His chest burned and filled with raw, stinging bliss.

THE VAN

Swayed off the highway and onto the grass, dirt kicking up, and the tires bouncing and skidding. Mackey squeezed his eyes open and tightened his grip on the steering wheel, letting his foot off the brake, swerving up the hilly embankment back onto the highway, the tires sliding across the loose gravel and dirt on the pavement, the ass-end fishtailing across the lanes. Chris jumped up and put his hands on the dashboard and SCREAMED.

Mackey regained control of the wheel and his breathing—

JONATHAN

Broke away from Elizabeth and retched, his chest heaving and regurgitating a long, thick line of phlegm. His throat contracted in spams. The world spinning and splitting in and out of darkness. He twisted and knotted his body, attempting to regain equilibrium and grapple against the drug which ripped at his heart and lungs and sucked the very breath from his mouth. His legs wobbled as he ran through the crowds of kids, and out the exit. Through the small crowded clusters outside the club. The outside world shrinking and collapsing, the stars dimming and shredding the sky, convulsing, and Jonathan turned the corner and tripped into a side alley and fell on his knees. The pebbles dug into his kneecaps. He rolled on his side, the pain not registering. The heart spasm and sudden bullet shot pain pounding the upper chest cavity forcing tiny, asthmatic puffs of air, and Elizabeth appeared above him talking words he could not understand, but heard the soaring engines of a plane swooping through the sky, and his mouth moved soundlessly, muttering

i can't see you—

you're

g o n e . . .

AT THE BEACH

Symphony rolled over and Troy grabbed her chest and played with her breasts. She slipped his hand away, laughed, and told him to knock it off. The digital clock flashed 4:00am. She realized she didn't know the time of day or the day of the week, but the dawn sky crept over the black, washing away the stars, blotting out the darkness.

Troy relaxed. His body coming alive. Again.

AT THE CABIN

The still lake. The wooden pier. A paddle boat tied to the post.

Inside, Chris slept sitting up on the couch. MTV's "120 minutes" echoed through the quite home. Mackey sat at the kitchen table, counting his money, separating the bills, smoothing each one flat. His knapsack on the chair. The plastic bag filled with a few hundred individually bagged Ecstasy tablets, and a couple of bundles of heroin, at the center of the table.

Victor lay sleeping in the guest room, supine position, arms out. Heather was in the shower, right off the guest room.

Mackey rose from his seat and stretched his arms above his head, way high. Big yawn. Big stacks of bills. A hand covered his mouth. A gun, with a silencer at the end, pointed to his temple. The cold steel nose made Mackey's eyes widen. A biker, red handkerchief covering the bottom half of his face, whispered in his ear

You're gonna hold still while my friend works, okay? You move, you don't see the sunrise over that pretty little lake.

His eyeballs shuddered and teared.

Another biker, a skull handkerchief covering his mouth, crept in from the sliding glass door behind them, and slid all the money and drugs into a garbage bag. Another biker, short yet powerfully built, walked over to the sleeping Chris and pointed a sawed-off shotgun at his face. Chris's eyes slowly peeled open. The barrel. The vacuous hole, dark and voidlike, stared him down. A whining gasp squeaked out his throat

SHHHHHHHHHHHHHHHHHHHHHHHHHHHHHH, said the biker. His long, thick mustache covered his lips, and the top half of his chin. Just two birdlike eyes, unflinching, filled with hate, penetrated the darkness of the den.

The biker with the skull handkerchief, bag in one hand, gun in the other, strode through the house, inching his way around the hallway to the first door on the right, the guest bedroom.

Mackey begged the biker not kill him. They could take anything they wanted; his aunt didn't keep anything of value in her summer home. And the biker laughed and said

We'll decide what's valuable or not. You just keep your fuckin mouth closed, okay darlin?

Water came from both ends: his crying eyes and pissed filled pants.

CHRIS

Shook, watching the piss drain from Mackey's pants and splash up against the floor.

Why's ya face so fucked up? asked the biker.

Chris wouldn't answer.

I asked ya a question, ugly.

Chris' face twitched and teared as he said, An accident.

Must've been some goddamn accident.

The bikers laughed, but kept it low.

THE SKULL FACED BIKER

Found the guest room. Placed down the bag. Turned the handle. Raised the silencer and placed his shoulder on the door. He pushed into it and the hinges creaked, like a nail being pulled from a rotted board. Victor jumped up, hands out. Yelled. The biker jumped back, aimed the pistol, squeezed the trigger, and a bullet ripped through Victors chest, splattering blood across the wall. He dropped instantly limp, tongue out, eyes wide open. The shower shut off. Skullface tiptoed to the bathroom. Peeked inside. Fogged bathroom mirrors. Heather was drying herself off. He watched her ass. The way it separated. Her calves, the way they flexed. The thickness of her cunt. He took step forward and said, I'm Tony, and she whirled around, screamed, dropped the towel, arms flailed and wavered and he hit her across the face with the butt of the pistol—

The other bikers heard the screams and the sawed-off shotgun fired a round into Chris' face, blowing the back of his head out. Chunks of brain splashed over the couch and in the kitchen he pulled the trigger against Mackey's temple and he dropped onto the table, flipping it over.

IN THE BATHROOM

Tony shattered the mirror with her head, then ripped her to the floor and bashed her face into the tile. He straddled her ass, pulled back his fist and hammered it into her spine. She choked, gasped, and her eyeballs flipped into her skull and he yelled its all clear and the other two bikers came in and dragged her to the guest room. She peered up at Victor's corpse and the blood on the wall and whimpered, squealed, cursed, and spit, and Tony removed his handkerchief and gagged her with it and licked his lips and called to Steve who already had her mounted, and called to Butch who smoothed his mustache first then grabbed her by the hair and pulled her up, shoving his cock down her throat, and Steve jammed himself in the other end of her and her ass clenched and legs twisted and he drove another fist into her spine

HOLD STILL, YA LITTLE PIG

And Steve continued to fuck her and she soon passed out and Butch slapped her a few times and her mouth moved but they couldn't revive her so they continued to fuck her as she lay unconscious on the rug, bleeding from the head and mouth and Steve laughed and shot his load across her back. Tony shoved Butch aside and shoved his cock in her mouth but he couldn't get hard and Butch laughed and slapped his back and told him to use his gun if he couldn't get it up ya old softie and Tony told him to shut the fuck up and zipped it back up. Steve said let's go, it's over and Butch hocked a loogie and let it dribble over her back and the sun rose over the lake and through the windows, shining off the thick pools of blood in the kitchen and den and the three walked out back and into the woods on the side of the cabin and hopped on their bikes and walked them through a trail which lead to a back road as the light filtered through the tree tops and the engines roared to life as the sun followed them down the highway…

AT THE BEACH

The sun rose over the Great South Bay and Symphony looked out and saw Fire Island across the water and her eyes teared and she smiled and Troy awoke and looked out the passenger window and saw the swing-set he used to go on when he was kid. He watched the sunbeams create images of children laughing and playing and they're happy and he smiled and his eyes got wet and Symphony reclined back, looking through the sunroof at the hard blue April sky and shut her lids.

SYMPHONY SLEPT.

MARIGOLD

SEGUE #3

CHAPTER 6
MOTEL MADNESS

THE ROOM LIT ONLY by the sunlight. The yellow walls. The frayed rug. The Blessed Mother hung on the yellow wall behind the bed. Poor Ophelia, no older than twelve, just couldn't hold back the tears, no matter what, but the older girl, Lisa, kept at it, each beat of the song, each girl with clasped hands, slapping them together harder and harder:

Bo-bo ski watten tatten,

Ah-ah-ah, boom boom boom

They sang quicker, and their clapping rhythm accelerated…

Itty bitty watten tatten

Bo bo ski watten tatten

Bo bo ski watten tatten

Freeze

Please

American Cheese

Please don't show your eyes to me.

Lisa covered her eyes and then shot her face forward and smiled.

Poor Ophelia cried and cried and groaned and cried some more and Lisa held her, shushing her and rocking her and placing gentle kisses on her forehead.

I miss my Mommy… and my puppy, said Ophelia in a whisper. I just wanta go home.

Lisa rocked her some more.

I'm scared, whispered Ophelia. We can run away. I know you want to.

You know you have my favorite name in the whole world, said Lisa in a thick NY/Spanish accent. OPHELIA. It's the most beautiful name I ever heard.

She sniffled and wiped the tears away with her arm. She tried to smile, tried so very hard, but the sadness was there, and it would not go away, no matter what.

I wish that was my name… you know that?

Ophelia stared at her bare feet, each reseted below an opposing knee, crossed Indian style. She traced a finger along the soles.

I think your name is real pretty, too. I like Lisa, she said, sniffling, coming down from the cry.

Yeah, that's not my real name though. Not even the johns know my real name.

Why?

Because fuck them, that's why. They don't need ta know, she said, pushing the long curls off Ophelia's face. They don't *deserve* ta know.

If it's a secret, I won't tell anyone if you tell me, she whispered.

Lisa thought about it and got real close to her lips and asked, Promise?

They both raised a pinky and hooked them together.

Promise. Now tell me your name?

Marielle.

THUMP THUMP THUMP…

Ophelia! Let's go! said the Man from the other side of the door. His voice— an indignant baritone, filled with urgency.

PART FOUR
MARIELLE

CHAPTER 7
JESUS SAVES

MARK 10:13:16

13 People were bringing little children to Jesus for him to place his hands on them, but the disciples rebuked them. 14 When Jesus saw this, he was indignant. He said to them, "Let the little children come to me, and do not hinder them, for the kingdom of God belongs to such as these. 15 Truly I tell you, anyone who will not receive the kingdom of God like a little child will never enter it." 16 And he took the children in his arms, placed his hands on them and blessed them.

MARIELLE came up in the system. Bronx born. Mom had her at 15, which meant she never finished school and had to work, but no job ever paid enough. So she got help from the state. Down to DSS for food stamps, rental assistance, and daycare. They appointed her a case manager who'd visit the home bi-weekly, to help manage her life. Marielle ran to him and hugged his legs, blew him kisses, drew him pictures. Had a bloody nose once. Wiped it on his pants accidentally after a hug. I have a cold, she said. Another time the lip was swollen and cracked and told him nothing, gave no reason, but tugged his hand and led him into the bedroom where she showed him an elaborate display of pictures she painted. Ugly, monstrous faces. Screaming, sharp teeth, big hands—RAISED, blood dripping from eyes and smiles and the case manager saw enough. Called CPS. Takes a few days for them to get there. In the meantime, Mom stepped on her neck and beat her fists into her back so bad she ended up getting spinal surgery. She was only twelve. CPS removed her from the home. They sent her to foster care and those parents didn't give a shit about her. Marielle would scream and cry and throw tantrums on the daily, and threaten to kill herself and they'd say, go ahead, go lay down in the middle of the tracks and let a train run right through ya, ya little fuckin brat. And those words fucked her up. She believed them. She'd go across the street and visit the park, just to escape mental bedlam. Watched the kids playing there with parents; kissing, holding, caressing, brushing the hair from their face, picking them up when they fell, and she'd watch and smile, and sit on the spinning wheel and whirled faster and faster. Some weekends she'd spend riding the subway with a few friends. Going nowhere in particular, just riding, laughing, teasing, and alluding. As she hopped off, a kid her age came up to her, selling sweets.

The man over there says ta pick whatever ya want.

Why?

The boy shrugged. She grabbed a Mallow Mars and by the time she looked up, there he stood before her.

You gonna say thank you? snapped the man, joking.

Marielle just stared at him.

I'm Mal. Whass your name?

She told him.

Why I always see youse on the subway for? Ya'll causin problems, bein all loud.

Ain't causin shit.

Damn, why so mean?

Marielle backed up against the subway wall, tossing her big head of curls from one side to the other.

Got that mean-ass Latina look ta ya.

What you think'a me is none'a my business. Keep it ta yourself, she snapped.

Ahhhhhhhhhhhhhhhhhh, they no good ta you at home? Huh?

Marielle turned away and walked toward the stairs.

I know sumptin about that.

Whatchu need ta know that for? You don't pay my bills. You don't need ta know nuttin. Bye.

She walked up the stairs, into the sunlight of the city, blotting her from his view. Mal followed. He took out a wad of cash.

Here! Here-here-here-here! he said, tugging her arm. When she turned, he smoothed out two twenty dollar bills and told her to open her hand.

Don't be takin no subways home. Take a cab, he said while walking away.

Marielle stared at the bills and yelled THANK YOU. He raised a hand and smiled. Marielle stepped at the edge of the sidewalk and watched the cabs roar by.

Don't even know how ta hail a cab, said Mal, shaking his head.

He stepped in the street and placed two fingers between his teeth and whistled. A few roared by, but one pulled up. He pulled out a card and slid it into the pocket of her jeans. Said to call him. And she did. The card stated he owned a used car dealership out in Queens, close to where she lived. He was twenty-three. Just ten years older than her. Each time he'd call, the excitement filled her groin and warmed her chest. His voice soothing; calm. Picked her up in a big, black Cadillac. She never seen a car so beautiful. He took her places. Bought her things. Nice little sweaters. The skirts, pants, and leggings all the girls wore in '91. Anything from fashion mags she had. Gold jewelry, Gucci, leather handbags, sunglasses, diamond earrings—heart shaped, pink encrusted diamond necklaces, and her foster Mom, Carol, yelled and hollered, to take this shit back! Ya look like a whore!

HORRIBLE, MEAN OLD WOMAN! YA TOLD ME TA THROW MYSELF IN FRONT OF A TRAIN! HOW COULD YOU SAY THAT?! YOU WANT ME DEAD?! YOU WANT ME

OUT OF YOUR LIFE?! YOU THINK YOUR LIFE WILL BE BETTER WITH ME NOT IN IT?!

Carol stood silent, mouth hung open like a zombie.

TELL ME! TELL ME HOW YA REALLY FEEL—CAROL! TELL ME TELL ME TELL MEEEEEEEEEEEEEEEEEEEE— I'LL LEAVE, JUST SAY IT—SAY IT!

Carol closed her mouth, turned about face, and walked out of the kitchen. Mascara tears bled from the eyes, caked in the corners, dribbling down in tiny clumps.

Mal picked her up from the park. He took her away to the Florida Keys. Took her to all the beaches. He made her feel like a STAR. Marielle couldn't believe how well he treated her. You don't need ta go back there if they don't care whether you live or die, he told her, and she never returned to that foster home again. He gave her very own room; everything pink, and everything felt BEAUTIFUL.

But he'd leave for days, and she'd be alone in the apartment. His cousins, friends would show up unannounced with new girls each week. When Mal returned she finally asked what the fuck business he really had, he told the truth

They're pimps, and them girls are theirs. Look, I ain't got no reason ta lie ta you.

And she believed him. Flew back to NY. Set up the operation in Queens. He took care of her. Caressed her, brushed the hair from her face, baby kissed her forehead; and shortly after, the instructions came, things she had to do with the johns and for how long, the many positions, how to fuck them, how to suck them, how to talk to them, how much to charge, and the right words to use so they'd give her more money. Work began at 9 a.m. and she'd go till 9 p.m., sometimes midnight. Some men laughed at her because she cried and she forced her eyes to shut and imagined herself somewhere else beyond the clouds in a warm place beneath the sun, and there was a friend there, Miranda, a friend she drew from her imagination that would help her and calm her and kiss her eyes and tell her it's okay and they'd be at peace in the sun. She kept her eyes shut so she wouldn't feel anything, see anything, but the banging, and banging and banging, the bed hammering against the wall, rattling the picture of the Blessed Mother that hung there. She'd stare into Mary's eyes and ask for help.

Several towns around Long Island and Queens. The brothels, the motels, the truck stops, certain streets known for prostitution, and even private homes. No days off. No holidays. 10 to 20 customers a day, seven days a week. She'd bleed, and throb, and hurt and Mal screamed at her.

WORK ON THROUGH!

One day a john gave her a couple of love bites on her neck. Muthafucka went too far. Mal beat her with a chain on her body, knotted her face with his fists, kicked her in the ribs, heard a snap but kept going, pulled her hair, spat in her face, and burned her stomach with an iron. She screamed and told him she wanted to leave and he accused her of falling in love with a customer. He told her she was being a whore. Twisted her arm, sprained her wrist. She had to work on through it.

YOU WANNA BE A FUCKIN WHORE, DONCHU?

Marielle tried to evade him. Many times. Many, many fucking times. Going to get some smokes. Going to get some food. Ya ain't goin nowhere bitch, back over here. Whatchu need, I'll get it. Sit yo ass down, nigga. Had one of his cousins sit by her door after her last john, during the few hours she had to sleep, shower, and get herself pretty for the next client at dawn. She stared at the Blessed Mother hung on the wall. Yelling, sometimes screaming at her.

YA DIRTY ROTTEN CUNT! YOU DON'T SEE THIS?! YOU BLIND! YOU DON'T HELP ME?! YOU AIN'T GOT SHIT WIT YO ROTTED EYES. THEY DON'T BLEED NO BLOOD! I AIN'T SEEN SHIT!

Only divine thing Marielle knew was her friend in the sun, Miranda. Miranda. Sweet Miranda. Dancing in the rings of the sun, the fire of the earth, the life of our breath. She hadn't seen her in a long while. Nothing but darkness when she'd shut them lids as the johns fucked her. And when things got tight, and Mal felt sketchy, they'd move again. A Motor Lodge on the island in Suffolk County. A motel with a reputation for prostitution. She closed her eyes during the worst john she'd had in months. Licking her mouth, her tiny earlobes and the baby hairs on the sides of her face. His dirty nails scratching her thighs, his mouth had a hot, bitter taste of an infected tooth. MIRANDA CAME with the sun in her eyes and all was golden aglow, soothing the little angel, touching her face, caressing her back, and the shouts from the other rooms, the moaning, the yelling and SCREAMING

POLICE!

POLICE!

EVERYONE OUT, LET'S GO, EVERYONE OUT!

Miranda you've done it! Goddam girl, I knew it. I knew to you came to me for a reason. I didn't put you in my head; you were born there, in the light of my eyes.

The police shut down the Motel. My lucky stars, I thank all of them, and the biggest star, the sun. They've come to rescue me and the other girls.

THE TEARS, THE TEARS OF FALLEN JOY

25 officers escorted Marielle and the girls to different rooms, closed out the main entrance and placed the leather duffle bags in the center of the rooms.

—THE BAGS UNZIPPED

—VIDEO CAMERAS REMOVED

The largest cop stepped forward in Marielle's room. Three other girls sit around her.

Okay, listen up ya little fuckin whores. See this camera here? This is God, ya understand? This sees all. Ya open ya mouths and it goes right to ya families. Now, remember… we found ya's here and it was no accident. That means we know more about ya's than ya think.

Disgusting cops. They knew they were minors. Oldest girl was Marielle at 14. Most were 10. And it began. Beds banging against the walls from the other rooms, the cries, the laughter, the screams — echoing dull thuds, the crying—the little girls CRYING!!!! The Blessed Mother banging against the wall. Her eyes staring, HER EYES!!!! A fat slobbering cop pounced on her, shaking the bed. His smelly mustache. Cigarettes and spit and onions and she gagged twice. It only lasted a minute. Beads of sweat fell from his brow and burned her eyes and blackened them out.

Maranda stood before her in tears and said:

Your sad dark eyes
Your sad brown liquid eyes
They bleed before Christ
Before the Virgin Mary herself
They bleed tears in fiery summits
Dance dance dance in the rings of the sun

SIX MONTHS LATER…

Marielle fell ill. The sour stomach. The vomiting. The headache as if someone pressed two thumbs into her eyeballs. The Listerine shots before and after each client. The pain, shooting from the uterus to the center of her belly. Told Mal. He got her a test at Rite Aid. Positive. Later on that year, after her 15th birthday, Marielle gave birth to a girl. Plastic drop cloths covered the motel floor, catching the afterbirth. She named her Nikki. And Mal used her daughter as the chain he beat her with if she didn't comply with his wishes.

I'LL KILL THIS LITTLE BITCH RIGHT HERE

Nikki stayed in a separate room and was cared for by the cousins. She'd see her baby twice a day. Once in the morning to feed and rock her, and once at night, after the last client until she never saw her again. She screamed and begged Mal to bring her back, but the beatings got worse and he gave her more clients, sometimes up to 20 a day, 7 days a week. And she cried and cried and cried until the tears stopped coming, until the cries dried up in her heart and her eyes blanked over, gazing to the void, waiting for nothing. Knowing there's nothing. The stare— a hollow meditation until the next client. And he ripped through her. Young guy, 20's, hammered in her and wouldn't stop. Even after he came. Banged the bed against the wall. The Blessed Mother staring down at her, doing NOTHING. But banging against the wall.

Her crotch began throbbing. A slow, burning throb, that increased each day and spread to her pelvis and lower back. Her legs trembled and twisted each time she'd urinate. Just the thought of feeling the bladder fill made her cry, knowing that sharp burn would follow. She begged Mal to take her to the ER. Begged for some medicine.

YOU FUCKIN THESE NIGGAS WITHOUT A CONDOM?

Mal pummeled her with punches, knotting her face and neck, splitting her chin. She begged for him to stop, that the throbbing between her legs made it impossible to take on a client.

IF YOU CAN'T USE YO CUNT, THEN USE YO MOUTH AND ASS.

My face is burnin… lemme see a doctor, said Marielle, lying on the bed, her legs convulsing.

He grabbed her by her t-shirt and yanked her up and said with his teeth, YOU'LL USE YO MOUTH. Mal twisted the front of her t-shirt and the collar squeezed her neck like a noose. She soon passed out. Mal and his cousin Lonny visited her an hour later.

Yo, sir, sir! Her face is burnin up, said Lonny.

Go see if Dequan has some leftover antibiotics from when he had strep.

You got it, boss.

Lonny left. Mal stayed with Marielle, glaring, eyes stuffed with hate and abject pity.

Her face turned a pale grey. He cracked a window for her. The wind blew her hair and she looked up, the sun rays slicing through the overcast sky; the rings of light scintillating outward from the gloom.

Lonny returned with a pill bottle and said, Only gotta couple left.

Whatta ya lookin at me for? Give'm ta her.

Lonny sat next to Marielle on the bed and handed her 2 capsules. She swallowed them without any water and lay back down, fetal position, facing the window.

She ain't look too good, boss. I'd leave'a alone for about a day or two, at least.

Lonny left the pill bottle on her nightstand. Mel left and let the door slam behind him. Lonny sat awhile, looking after her, and then finally left; his eyes swollen with tears.

The clouds burned off by late afternoon and Miranda appeared before her.

C'mon. We're goin somewhere…

She took her by the hand and led her through a wooded trail of vines. The unseen waves echoed and hit the shoreline like claps of thunder. Marielle smiled. Her heart raced—

A HEAVY *THUMP THUMP THUMP* on her door.

Mal peeked his head in, Yo, how you feelin?

Marielle turned and faced him, A little better.

Okay, cos I got clients here, yknow? And if *that* ain't still feelin good, ya still can do other things, yknow what I'm sayin.

A tall, gangly gentleman of 40 stood behind Mal. Pus-filled boils covered his face and neck. He walked in and removed his truckers cap. Nodded. Mal vanished behind the door. It closed SHUT. He sat beside her on the bed. Smiled.

How are ya, darlin? he said with a southern drawl.

I'm fine.

You are purdy.

Thank you, said Marielle softly.

He tugged on her finger and smiled again. She wouldn't look at him. After a few moments, he stood and released a sigh of frustration.

The UNBUCKLING BELT

The UNZIPPING FLY

I'mma minute man… witta face like that? Shiiiiiiit… I ain't lasting too long, girly.

He pushed his underwear aside and pulled it out. Marielle crawled across the bed and reached for it. A sudden aroma whooshed up her nostrils of diesel, sweat, and a warm, almost feline odor. She held in her breath and took it all in her mouth, letting it slid down the back of her throat. The technique acquired for the ugly ones so they'd finish quickly. She twisted the hand and mouth in motion, pulling toward the head. A violent retch heaved inverted her spine, the temples throbbed, still feverish, the flank pain still dull, and within minutes, MINUTES!!! the cum slithered down her throat. She closed her eyes, closed off the taste, and looked up at him and forced a smile. The man teetered back, legs shaking, expressionless and void, he pulled his pants up, grabbed his hat and walked to the door. Not a nod, wink, or shiver, and he was gone. Marielle felt her throat contract and mouth fill with saliva. She ran to the bathroom and vomited several times. Brushed, washed her mouth out, retched again, and took the last two antibiotics. She slid down her shorts and under-wear. It still hurt. Two fingers swabbed the insides. Grey discharge. Her hands shook. The fear burned and tickled from her bowels up to her belly.

THE NEXT DAY…

Ophelia came to visit. She curled up next to her in bed.

You still wanta be a nurse someday? asked Ophelia.

She nodded yes, clutching her hand.

That's very nice. I wanta do something nice one day too, but I can't decide on what. I turn fourteen tomorrow and Mal said he gettin me brownies. When I blow out the candles I will wish and hope and pray I find what I'm meant for. And I will wish and hope and pray for you to get better. Okay?

Marielle nodded yes, and kissed Ophelia's knuckles.

. . .

Early the next morning, Marielle heard Mal screaming at Ophelia from the other room. The walls muffled their voices. She barely made out the words. Too sick to move, her eyes remained on the ceiling, trying to create shapes and patterns from the various cracks. Ophelia must've not wanted to work on her birthday. The bed banged against the wall. Things broke against the floor. The screams penetrated the motel walls, climbing in octaves, higher and higher. Marielle turned to the Blessed Mother, covered both ears, and it's a scream she's heard many times before; a scream she's become accustomed to, but this time the screams are choking, clotting, falling apart, breaking, BREAKING against the floor.

THUMP THUMP THUMP…

Then silence. Heavy breathing. Mal shooting his mouth off. Giving someone directives. The voices became more discernible as they go down the hall and the other doors opened and closed and some other girls cried, and squealed and groaned and Mal told them to shut the fuck up and get back in your room and Marielle, too weak to move, laid there passively in a sweaty mass. Even an inch of movement caused pain in the skin, a flu-like pain. The sheets hurt. Her soft, white t-shirt hurt, and sent shivers and tiny shocks all over her body. Mouth pasted shut. Throat throbbed. Water. Water—

The footsteps pounding up and down the hall. MISERABLE pounding. Time hanging on her back like a monkey. Each minute like an hour. Time just sucking her blood. So slow. Too slow. She missed when time just flew by and it was summer, flew by and it was fall, and Christmas, and so forth and so on. Now it pulsed and she felt every second. Every miserable second. The monkey wouldn't let go. Biting her ear. gnawing it right the fuck off. Tearing her down. Too slow. Getting up in her guts. The hot, dull throb there. First the temples, then the glutes, pelvis, back up to the head. She looked to the window. When will the clouds go away? When will my stomach stop throbbing. When will Mary answer me? Why won't she ever hear me. Time needs to happen and speed up and the body needs to get healing. There's no more time for slow time. Antibiotics needed to work faster.

I'm a scream without a throat. A cry without a sound........

She soon slept.

GET THE FUCK UP said Mal.

One eye opened and the bleary light pierced straight to the back of her eyeball and the pressure swelled, as if two thumbs were digging them out.

TAKE THESE, he said, handing her four capsules and a glass of water.

She took them, drank the water.

WEAR DIS, he said dropping a pair of jean shorts and crop top on the bed. GOT PEOPLE COMIN BY TA LOOK AT YA.

Marielle slipped the jean-shorts on while Mal watched. A drop of blood leaking out from her crotch, bleeding down her thigh. She quickly rubbed it away with a finger. Mal glanced out the window, then left. She sat at the end of the bed. Sunlight leaked in, warming her thighs. She waited for Miranda; her smiling, beautiful brown face aglow with all the light in the world, all the light in the universe, all of everything wrapped smugly inside the most perfect and radiant goddess ever put forth in all creation— Miranda, Miranda, sweet Miranda. She is the divine, the holy trinity, the alpha and omega, and she is the reason I push through the tired exhaustion and face the grayness of the dying day.

A surge of energy filled her chest, arms, and legs. She jerked her head up. Her eyes, hot and wet, bounced and shook as if the Holy Spirit finally found a place in her bones, a sanctum for rejuvenation and hope. Her jaw ground down on her teeth, and the pain of her bowels and pelvis soon subsided and the door flung open and Mal stepped in with Joey and Steve and told her to get her sweet little ass up on the bed and stand, twirl around, bounce a little, move it around a little.

SHE A BOTTOM BITCH, DIS ONE HEA.

Joey ran a hand over his long, greasy hair. Steve watched, mesmerized by her moving, twisting, bouncing, and flicking her tongue, licking around her lips. She stretched a leg out and thick stream of blood ran down the inside thigh. Steve saw and said what's up? Thought she looked sick, and Mal said no, no, no, she's okay. Look at her. She look sick to you?

Tryna unload a sick one, aye? said Steve.

Ya, ya, "bottom bitch," aye, said Joey. Tryna unload a sick one. C'mon, we're out.

Joey and Steve left and Mal shouted at Lonny to show them one more down at room 13, but they refused, and their voices were clear and strong and rang like a bell and Mal slammed the door shut behind him, and grabbed her by the hair and dragged down from the bed. She fell sideways, landing on her shoulder, and something popped inside it, pushing into her jaw, forcing her mouth to bite through the tongue. The Blessed Mother fell from the wall and cracked in half. Her left leg kicked out and hit Mal's ankle, and he punched her on the back of the head. Her face hit the floor; she clasped her fingers over her head, and he punched through the knuckles and split the scalp— blood gushed. He entwined his hand through her hair, dragged her across the floor, her legs kicked and wheeled and she rolled over as the sunlight streamed in, thick bars of it, and Marielle reached out and Miranda took her by the hand, still trudging through the wooded trail of vines, and the waves echoed and hit the shoreline like claps of thunder and Marielle smiled and the vines peeled apart, and the trail gave way to the ocean and Miranda turned and smiled and kissed her forehead—

An ugly boot unturned her face and the front teeth broke apart in her mouth and a knife cut through the jugular and Miranda pulled her though THROUGH through!!!! and the sand, THE BILLIONS OF TINY GRAINS glimmered off the sun like broken shards of glass, and the blood drained from her body and she stared out of the window into the rings of the sun, her eyes wide as skies.